THE GREAT GASTON MURDER

PENELOPE BANKS MURDER MYSTERIES
BOOK 6

COLETTE CLARK

DESCRIPTION

A glitzy party to end the summer with a bang… that ends with an even bigger bang.

New York 1925

It's Penelope "Pen" Banks's twenty-fifth birthday and she is throwing a summer party that would leave even Gatsby himself in awe.

Upon arriving early to the Long Island mansion where it's to be held, she discovers a young, handsome artist has taken up residence in one of the cottages on the property. There are secrets and suspicions surrounding James Gaston's arrival, including the nearby murder of a maid from another estate across the bay.

Still, there's something about the young man that encourages Pen to help him in his endeavor to win back his long-lost love, most notably his mysterious relationship with the original owner of the Long Island home, Agnes Sterling.

Amid love triangles, bitter rivalries, class warfare, and cryptic relationships, another murder occurs the night of Pen's party. Now, with the help of Detective Richard

Prescott, she must discover the true motives behind each murder in order to find justice for the dead.

The Great Gaston Murder **is the sixth book in the Penelope Banks Murder Mysteries series set in 1920s New York. The enjoyment of a historical mystery combined with the excitement, daring, and danger of New York during Prohibition and the Jazz Age.**

AUTHOR'S NOTE

Almost every high school student in the United States (and perhaps other countries?) is familiar with the F. Scott Fitzgerald book, *The Great Gatsby*. Since it was published the same year that Penelope Banks began her soon-to-be illustrious career as a private investigator, I had no choice but to include a murder mystery that put a fine little spin on it. Rest assured, there is no plagiarism here, just a bit of poetic license taken with the framework.

I usually include my Author's Note at the end of the novel, detailing the research that I put into a book. But there is only one source for the little tidbits you'll find in this book. Rather than give away the Easter eggs and twists I put on the classic, I'll allow you the fun of picking them out yourself.

You needn't have read *The Great Gatsby* in order to appreciate this murder mystery. Though, out of professional courtesy to the author who provided the inspiration, it behooves me to encourage you to do just that.

Happy reading!

CHAPTER ONE

LONG ISLAND 1925

"It's lucky for you I don't have a gun!"

Penelope "Pen" Banks brandished the cattails in her hand as she stared at the young man, her bright blue eyes wide with warning. He had appeared out of the blue from the cottage on the grounds of the mansion here in Glen Cove. The Long Island property had once belonged to a dear friend of her deceased mother's, Agnes Sterling. Penelope had arrived to prepare for the birthday party she was hosting this coming Saturday.

"Yes, I suppose it is a good thing you don't have a gun. Though, I must admit those cattails look awfully daunting," he said cautiously, keeping his hands raised as she had demanded.

"Are you teasing me?" Pen had to admit she did feel rather silly holding such a strapping young man at bay with nothing more than local flora.

"Not at all, ma'am. But perhaps you'll allow me to explain before you attack me with those things."

"It sounds like you're teasing me again."

"Have you seen what cattails do when they break open? I'd like to do us both a favor and prevent that if I could. At the very least, may I put my hands down?"

As though he even needed to ask. He could easily tackle her to the ground if he chose to.

"Slowly," Pen warned. "And no sudden moves!"

"Yes ma'am."

"And stop calling me 'ma'am.' You make me feel like a prudish schoolmarm."

After all, in a few days she'd only be twenty-five; not *terribly* old. Certainly not old enough for something as ill-fitting as "ma'am."

"Sorry...miss?"

"That'll do," Pen said, feeling herself relax at his self-effacing response. He really didn't look all *that* threatening and at least kept a respectful distance. "I suppose I can't fault you for squatting in one of the empty cottages. It does seem rather a waste for all this property to go unused."

"Squatting?" he repeated, looking perplexed. "You've got it wrong, miss. Miss Sterling gave me an open invitation to stay in one of the cottages."

Mentioning Agnes had Pen sharpening her gaze. Perhaps he wasn't squatting after all. Agnes did like picking up strays, mostly of a certain ilk, which meant only one thing.

"You're an artist?"

"I am," he replied, surprised she had guessed it.

Yes, he even had the look of an artistic stray. His brown, foppish hair was unfashionably long, curling around his ears and down to the middle of his neck. The loose white shirt and dark canvas pants gave him a certain roguish appeal, like a young pirate or provincial revolutionary.

He was probably quite popular with ladies interested in

THE GREAT GASTON MURDER

taking a risk with a handsome devil. Particularly with those stunning aquamarine eyes of his. They were perfectly mesmerizing pools that had Pen drawing in her claws even more.

Penelope could see why Agnes had given him an open invitation. Not that she had ever been the type to *consort* with her little projects. She did however have a good eye for talent and always trusted her gut about people, usually correctly.

Still, to be safe, Penelope would check with Chives, the butler she had de facto inherited from Agnes as well.

"Alright, I'll give you a chance to explain yourself."

One side of his mouth hitched up into a smile showing off a small dimple. Oh yes, this one was a charmer. Of course, Penelope had learned to be wary of charmers over the past year working as a private investigator. Still, there was something decidedly appealing about this young man.

As a matter of fact, there was something strangely familiar about him. Penelope traversed every inch of her memory, trying to land on a moment where she'd seen him before. The way her mind worked she could remember everything she'd seen as though in a colorized photograph.

The image standing before her had never been captured.

So why did he seem so familiar?

"My name is James Gaston, and yes I am an artist. I picked that cottage because it has the best view of the bay."

It was also the furthest away from the rest of the property, particularly the main house. All the better to go unnoticed. It didn't immediately make him suspect, particularly because he had a point about it being the one with the loveliest panoramic view of the water.

"Penelope Banks," she responded. "Just how long have you been staying there?"

"Only since this Saturday, so not even a week. I heard of Agnes's death earlier this year from Mr. Wilcox." Something flickered in his gaze, a certain regret or conflict. "I debated returning to New York to give my condolences, since I wasn't known to any of her friends."

"No, you aren't," Penelope said in a pointed way. Still, he *had* mentioned Mr. Wilcox, who had been Agnes's attorney, and was now Penelope's. Either he had done his research, or Agnes really had been his patron. "Just how is it you first came to know Agnes?"

"That's a somewhat involved story. It was through my mother, who used to work at a few of her parties."

Pen didn't care if it was "somewhat involved," she had plenty of time to hear about it. Still, the August heat was beginning to wear on her, particularly this late in the day.

"You might as well come inside. You can tell me over a drink," Penelope said dropping the cattails in her hand.

"If you insist," he said with another smile.

At least most of the essential staff had arrived so she wouldn't be alone with him in the main house. How he had escaped their notice, since they had come a few days ahead of her, was something she planned on inquiring about. Perhaps they thought he was *her* guest?

"Just how did you get past the front gate?" Penelope asked as they began walking toward the mansion.

"I didn't, not originally. Once you make it to the shore, it's rather easy to get access to any of these properties."

"So you just walked along the beach to get here?" she asked incredulously. The nearest easily accessible shoreline was at least a few miles away.

"At the time I only had my rucksack with me. It's not a

terrible walk. Once I was on the grounds, I opened the gate to have the rest of my belongings delivered to the cottage."

Penelope laughed despite herself. "You really are bold, aren't you?"

He grinned and shrugged. "As I said, Agnes did give me an open invitation to stay so long as it wasn't otherwise occupied. In all fairness, no one was here when I first arrived."

There was a mischievous nature about him that Pen felt a certain kinship towards. She herself had been known to go places she wasn't necessarily supposed to go, and getting there via means that weren't exactly sanctioned.

Since the pond where she found James was closer to the back of the mansion that faced the sound, Penelope took the back stairs. They led to the large terrace that overlooked Long Island sound. This weekend, the entire area, the main areas inside, and a good portion of the rest of the property would be filled with people, all there to celebrate her birthday. As much as Penelope was looking forward to it, she did also enjoy the quiet serenity of the moment.

They entered through the French doors into the large open foyer where the double spiral staircase led to the second floor of the house. Penelope escorted James to the right, heading towards the parlor which once served as the main bar area of the mansion before Prohibition. Technically, it *still* served as the main bar area. Agnes had never been a teetotaler or one to abide by silly laws, and neither was Pen.

"So what's your poison?" Penelope asked, removing her sun hat and smoothing down her dark bobbed hair.

She had invited friends to stay for the few nights leading up to the party. As such, Chives had made sure the bar had all the essentials and extras for any drink they'd be inclined to want. There was even champagne already on ice.

"Oh no, allow me," James insisted.

"You're the guest. I'm the one who should be hosting you."

"I'm the squatter," he said with a grin. "I should repay you for not attacking me with those cattails. In fact, I have a specific drink in mind, one that I learned to make while I was abroad."

"Well, now I'm too intrigued to say no. By all means, the bar is yours."

She took a stool and watched as he made his way around to the back of the bar.

"Whoever supplied you knew what they were doing."

"In these days of Prohibition, I should hope so. The markup on that hooch is criminal."

He laughed good-naturedly at her joke. It made his eyes sparkle in a way that warmed her insides. What was it about this man that struck something in her? Perhaps they had met as children and she didn't fully recognize him as an adult? Pen figured she might as well use this moment while he was busy making a drink to find out more about him.

"So again, how is it you know Agnes?"

He took hold of the champagne that had been chilling in the ice bucket and pulled it out. "You don't mind if I use this do you?"

It was enough to distract Penelope. She knew the bottle had been put on ice preemptively, but for no special reason. Still, using a perfectly good bottle of champagne to make a cocktail was rather audacious of him. But she was curious all the same. Maybe it would help her learn more about him. It wasn't as though she couldn't afford a hundred more with the amount Agnes had left her.

"If you must."

Something shifted in his expression, as though her blithe attitude toward the champagne confirmed something for him. Suddenly, she wondered who was doing the detective work here.

"You were about to tell me how you knew Agnes?" she asked again while his back was turned to reach for the gin.

"As I said, my mother met her first," he said, his back still turned to her. Penelope could see him in the mirrored glass. His eyes were deliberately focused on opening the bottle of gin as he answered. "She had been a fortune teller. Agnes had first hired her for one of her parties before I was ever born."

Penelope knew that Agnes had liked to bring in all sorts of performers. It's what made her parties so notorious. Penelope was employing the same event organizer that Agnes had used in the past. Hopefully, it would do her memory justice. A fortune teller made sense, but was still a rather tenuous connection to the man standing before her.

"You said she *had* been?"

Pen saw him pause for a moment before answering. "My mother died over three years ago."

"I'm sorry."

He shrugged. "It was an accident. I'm told she went quickly."

"Well, she must have been some fortune teller if Agnes hired her for a party."

James chuckled and he turned around, bringing the bottle of gin with him. Pen watched him pluck a few sugar cubes and put them into a shaker. He used the muddler to break them apart, then added the gin.

"That she was," he said as he reached for a lemon. "Mostly, she was a good read of people. It's all a performance, you see, no different from a magic show. In the case of fortune-telling, the sleight of hand and deflection are mental rather than visual. Get people talking, mostly about their past, it opens the door to a lot of things."

"Heaven forbid our futures should be determined by our pasts. In that case, my fortune is rather worrisome."

His expression didn't match her teasing tone as he looked down at the curl he was peeling off the rind of the lemon. "Unfortunately, most people's futures *are* dictated by their pasts."

"And then sometimes fortune strikes," Penelope said studying him.

His gaze snapped back to her, his eyes piercing her. A slow smile came to his face. "I certainly hope you're right, Miss Banks."

"Penelope."

"Penelope." He took a breath and a cloud seemed to lift from him as he cut the lemon in half and squeezed both sides into the shaker. "My mother was the one to reach out to Agnes once it became apparent that I had some talent as an artist. Or rather, it was that I had *no* talent being a performer as the rest of my family did."

"You come from a family of performers?" Penelope asked leaning in with heightened interest. "How fascinating! My mother was a performer—on the stage though. She worked in San Francisco, or so I've been told." Pen's mother, Juliette Banks, had died during the Great Influenza.

James smiled as he grabbed several ice cubes with tongs to add them to the shaker. "Well, it seems we have something in common. Though my family was in the carnival circuit, up and down the eastern coast."

"You grew up in a carnival? What fun!"

His smile faded. "One would think so. In reality, it's decidedly less enjoyable."

James began shaking the shaker and there was a pause as the noise of it prevented further discussion. When he was done, he reached for two glasses, champagne flutes, and strained the liquid equally into both of them until they were half filled. "As a child, of course, it was one big playground. You're doted on, at least until you're old enough to earn your keep. That's when you learn the reality of what carnival life is like, the dark underbelly."

"Are you telling me they aren't the trustworthy, upright members of society I've been led to believe they were?" Penelope said, hoping she wasn't offending him.

He laughed as he grabbed the champagne. "I had a feeling I would like you."

"Oh? So it wasn't when I was threatening you with cattails?"

He laughed again and winked. "Maybe I just have a bit of the eye like my mother did. I can tell you're good people."

He popped the champagne and Penelope's heart stalled at the noise of it. She watched him pour an amount into each glass until they were full, then he placed a curl of lemon on the edge of each.

"Voila!" he announced as he placed one glass before her. "I give you the French 75, or at least a recent version of it."

It certainly was pretty, Penelope had to give him that. She took a sip and was delighted at the taste, a little sour, a little sweet, with the perfect amount of gin and bubbles. "Well now, that's certainly worth opening a bottle of champagne."

James lifted his glass. "*À votre santé.*"

Penelope lifted her glass to him in response to the toast

spoken in perfectly accented French. "I take it Agnes sent you to France then?"

He lifted one eyebrow and smiled. "Paris. You should be a detective."

"I am," Penelope said hoping she didn't sound too smug. "A private investigator."

He set his glass down and studied her. "And here I thought I was the interesting one. How did you get into that?"

"You first," Penelope said through slightly narrowed eyes as she continued to drink. "You were supposed to be telling me about yourself so I can rest assured you aren't a vicious murderer."

He lowered his head in a conceding nod. "Of course. Well, I had a talent for art early on. I started by working on most of the signage at the carnival. Then, I'd use the leftover paint to make my own creations on whatever I could find to work on, spare lumber, old canvas tarps, and even empty bags of popcorn. Whatever town we were in, I'd escape to the local library to look through art books."

There was a pause as some part of him traveled back to those days, lingering on the memory of it with apparent fondness. He blinked it away and came back to the present.

"Fortunately, my mother saw something in me beyond just the grunt work I was forced into, since I was no good at anything particularly useful. She reached out to Agnes, and the rest is history."

Penelope mulled that over as they sipped their cocktails. It wasn't a *completely* implausible story. Agnes had found many a diamond in the rough in unusual ways. Pen reassured herself that she would confirm as much as she could with Chives and Mr. Wilcox. For now, she wanted to know more about James from his own mouth.

Having played cards to make ends meet for several years before she got her inheritance from Agnes, Penelope considered herself a decent reader of people. Then again, this man had grown up in the carnival, so he probably knew how to put on a good con. At the very least it would put her skills to the test.

"When was it *you* first met Agnes?"

"Almost five years ago, when I was eighteen." That made him about two years younger than Penelope. "She immediately sent me to Paris and got me settled there. I had to spend the first year just trying to learn French," he said with a laugh. "After that, I trained at a school and then under various apprenticeships until I developed my own style."

It was odd that Agnes would plant someone coming from such a background in Paris right away. After all, there was an impressive art community right there in New York in which he could have first become acclimated. Pen imagined going from the rather clannish milieu of the carnival straight to the cultural and art center of the world, all in a foreign language. It must have been quite the adjustment.

"And now you're back in the U.S."

His mouth formed a smile, but there was something that steeled his aquamarine eyes as he responded. "And now I'm back."

Before she could ask any more questions, the sound of the doorbell rang through the house. Penelope assumed it was another delivery for the upcoming party and ignored it, at least until a minute later when Chives appeared. His eyes briefly landed on James and his only reaction was a simple polite blink before he turned his attention to Penelope. As usual, with his professional demeanor, it was impossible to tell what Chives was thinking. Did he recognize James or not?

"Miss Banks, there's a police officer at the door."

That had both James and Penelope sitting up straighter in surprise.

"Really? What does he want?"

"It seems they have found the body of a young woman."

CHAPTER TWO

James joined Penelope at the front door to greet the police officer. Penelope had a somewhat tenuous history with the Glen Cove Police Department so she was pleased to note that this member of the department didn't seem to recognize her.

"Good morning, Miss Banks, is it?" he tipped his hat to her.

"Yes, that's right."

His eyes fell to James next to her and narrowed slightly, no doubt judging him by his clothing and longish hair. "And you are?"

"James Gaston."

"James is a guest of mine," Penelope said, then hurriedly continued on. "Please come in, let's speak in the sitting room."

"Oh, no ma'am, I don't want to take too much of your time. We're just making inquiries about a woman whose body we discovered early this morning. We think she may have been killed late last night."

"Yes, Chives mentioned that. What happened?"

"Well, we've finally been able to identify her. Martha Combs? It seems she worked as a maid for the Belmont family."

"I know the Belmonts. My understanding is that they've been in Newport the past few weeks. Also, their home is over in Sands Point. I wouldn't have thought that was Glen Cove's jurisdiction."

Sands Point was on the other side of the bay, where Old Money had built their summer homes. Glen Cove was a slightly more recent enclave of the wealthy, with much more land on which to build much more massive monuments to New Money such as the one they were in right now.

"You're correct ma'am. However, Mrs. Combs was killed here in Glen Cove."

"Really?"

"Yes, she was run over with a car sometime overnight not too far from here, on Brookline Drive." His eyes briefly darted to James before coming back to Penelope.

Penelope inhaled sharply, absorbing this news. "What was she doing on Brookline Drive?"

"That's one of the questions we're trying to answer. How many cars are on the property?"

"Only the one, driven by my chauffeur. Of course, there have been deliveries and such coming and going as well. None late last night, as far as I know."

"Can you think of any reason why Mrs. Combs might have been coming here? Maybe to visit with a member of the staff or as a guest?" Again his gaze briefly darted to James.

"I can't imagine that being the case. Most of the staff only just arrived in the past few days, and I arrived yesterday afternoon. I can certainly inquire with them to see if any of them knew her or had a reason for her to visit."

"Actually ma'am it would probably be best if the police handled the questioning."

"Of course."

"What time did you arrive in Glen Cove, Miss Banks?"

"Around 3 o'clock in the afternoon yesterday. And I can assure you that my driver didn't run over anyone on the way here."

"Of course ma'am. As I stated, it happened overnight." He shifted his attention to James. "And you?"

"I arrived Saturday...on foot."

The officer's brow rose. "On foot from where?"

"I took the train in and walked along the coast to get here from the station."

The officer steeled his gaze. "This is a serious police matter, no time for joking."

Penelope could understand the skeptical look on the officer's face. Being a guest at a house like this, one would expect a certain level of accommodation, at the very least a car and driver sent to pick him up. Someone taking it upon themselves to walk from the train station didn't make very much sense.

"I understand, and I'm not joking. I've been here on the estate the entire time, in one of the cottages. And I don't have a car."

"You said you arrived Saturday, so five days ago?" the officer continued, still looking suspicious.

"Yes, sir."

"You wouldn't happen to know or recognize Mrs. Combs, would you? She's about 5 foot 4, red hair, twenty-two years of age," he cleared his throat, before continuing, "attractive figure."

Penelope pursed her lips with wry distaste. The officer at least had the decency to look apologetic at the tawdry descriptor. Still, she supposed he had to be descriptive in a way that another man would appreciate.

"I'm sorry officer, that doesn't sound like anyone familiar to me."

"Have you met with *anyone* since you've been here? Perhaps someone came to visit you?"

"As I said, I've spent almost all my time alone in my cottage here. Mostly, I've been painting, I'm an artist."

The officer's expression reflected exactly what he thought of that. "Would anyone be able to confirm that you were here and alone last night?"

If anything, James seemed mildly amused rather than offended by the not-so-subtle accusation in the officer's voice. "No, I don't suppose they would. I'm terribly sorry for what happened to Mrs. Combs, and I do hope you find out who did this. However, I haven't even seen a woman with red hair, or one who fits that description since I've been here. In fact, I've been living in France for the past five years, so I don't know many people in New York at all."

Based on the officer's expression, this did nothing to improve his opinion of the young man.

"I see, well I suppose that's that." He didn't look entirely convinced, but there was only so much he could do with what James had told him. He turned his attention back to Penelope. "A detective will be by later to talk with your staff, but I'd like to inspect the car driven by your chauffeur."

"Of course, Chives can arrange everything. Is there anything else that you need from us?"

"I understand you're having a party this Saturday?"

"I am, and I made sure to give Chief Higgins plenty of

advance notice. I can assure you that I don't intend to cause any problems for the Glen Cove Police Department."

Penelope knew there had been an unspoken understanding between Agnes and the department when it came to the alcohol that was served at such parties. So long as they didn't have to handle any more serious crimes, and since every mansion in Long Island hosted similar parties all summer with similar violations of the Volstead Act, they usually looked the other way.

"Yes, of course, ma'am. I was just wondering if there might be some connection."

"Well, the handling of staff has been arranged well ahead of time. I wouldn't have needed to borrow the services of the Belmonts' maid. But again, you're free to question the staff to see if she was meeting with any of them. I still don't understand what she might have been doing on the road so far away from Sands Point in the middle of the night. That's rather odd."

"It is, particularly considering the circumstances surrounding the murder."

"Murder?" Penelope latched onto that word. "So you don't think it was an accident?"

"No ma'am," he said, with a hint of disgust in his voice.

"May I ask why?" Pen said, now even more curious.

"I'd rather not offend your sensibilities with the details, ma'am."

"Oh please, I'm not some wilting violet. I've certainly seen my fair share of death." Penelope realized that wouldn't do anything to present her in a good light, so she added a bit of feminine appeal. "If I'm in any danger, I believe I have a right to know exactly what sort of danger."

The officer studied her for a moment, briefly looked at James, then brought his attention back to her. "I probably shouldn't say, but I suppose you do have a right to know. It seems she was run over...multiple times."

Penelope reeled in horror. "Goodness."

"I'm sorry to have upset you, ma'am."

"No, no, I appreciate knowing all the facts. By all means, the staff is at your disposal."

"Thank you, ma'am."

Penelope called for Chives and left him to deal with the officer. She led James back into the parlor, feeling rattled by the details of Martha's murder. It certainly was a dark start to what should have been a celebratory weekend for her.

"It seems rather macabre to finish off the last of the champagne, now," James said, eyeing the bottle.

"The bottle is open, we might as well drink it before it goes flat," Penelope said taking her seat on the stool again. "Besides, I could use it after hearing that news."

James reached for the bottle and poured champagne into what was left in their glasses. Pen accepted hers and took a sip, eyeing him over the rim as he looked off to the side in deep thought. She swallowed and set her glass down.

"I also think it's time you told me the truth."

CHAPTER THREE

TO HIS CREDIT, JAMES DIDN'T LOOK SURPRISED AT Penelope's insinuation that he hadn't been completely honest with the police officer.

"What makes you think I was lying?" James asked, looking only mildly curious.

"I didn't say you were lying, but you weren't being entirely forthcoming either. You were awfully circumspect in your answer about having visitors. I know the mansion was empty when you first came. I have a feeling you didn't spend *all* that time alone."

Pen took a sip of her champagne as she waited for him to answer. There was still the lingering residue of French 75, which she actually would have preferred. Perhaps she could get James to make another after he told her everything. Then again she might not like what he had to say.

This business about Martha Combs being murdered was unsettling. If Penelope hadn't been introduced to so much murder in her newfound career, she might have been quite a bit more shaken and far less likely to sit so closely to a man who was still essentially a stranger.

As it was, she was willing to be open-minded without jumping to conclusions. Still, she couldn't rid herself of the idea that it was awfully coincidental that Martha should be murdered, and in such a deliberate manner, the same week that James decided to take up residence—after five years, supposedly spent abroad.

A slow, humorless smile spread his lips. "Yes, you're right, I was careful with my wording. I did in fact have company this week, but it wasn't Martha Combs or anyone who looks like her. I've never met her or even heard her name before today. And the person who came to visit came by boat, not by car. It would have been too risky with you already moved in, along with so much of the staff."

"So are you going to tell me who it was?"

His smile deepened, now looking almost bashful. "I had hoped to introduce this in a more graceful way. My return to the United States wasn't without a reason. I came back to see someone, someone from my past. She's staying here in Long Island this summer. Her name is Savannah Duncan."

Penelope searched her memory trying to place the name and nothing came to her. While she didn't know *every* family who summered in Long Island, she knew most of the wealthy ones from New York, having grown up in that world. Perhaps Savannah was another artist or maybe a member of the staff of one of the households?

If James really did grow up in a carnival setting, he certainly wouldn't have been introduced to society. Then again, most young ladies of society didn't necessarily limit their trysts to other members of the upper crust. James was certainly the kind of young man that would draw the eye of a socialite who wanted to rebel.

"She's from North Carolina," James said.

"But named Savannah," Penelope said with a wry smile.

James laughed softly. There was a certain innocent quality to it that reminded Penelope of the giggles she used to get when she was a girl swooning over some boy.

"We met when the carnival was just outside of Charleston one spring. We were both seventeen at the time. I had run off to the library as usual, and there she was looking at a book on Degas." He looked off to the side in wonder, as though seeing her for the first time again. "I never understood why she would give a boy like me a second glance. In fact, I had made sure to keep my distance, since I still had the stink of carnival sweat on me. But she looked right at me with those big blue eyes and asked without any hesitation or even introduction, 'Do you think he painted ballerinas so often because he was in love with one and couldn't be with her?' I'd been through enough books at that time to know Degas and what his favorite subject was. I was too dumb-struck to think of an intelligent answer. In fact, all I could think of was why this wonder had even acknowledged my existence. I just responded with the first thing that came to me, 'If he had, he probably wouldn't have made all those paintings and you wouldn't be here looking at that book. Then, I never would have met you.'"

"Not such a terrible answer."

"Well, it worked. From there, we'd meet in our small corner of the library to look at art books, or go to a museum. Any chance to sneak away where we could be alone. Like my folks, hers weren't big on art and whatnot. By the time the carnival was moving on, I already had a plan to come back once we both turned eighteen." He gave a rueful smile. "Actually, I didn't have any kind of a plan at all I just knew I was coming back."

Obviously, the star-crossed lovers didn't have their

happy reunion. Pen didn't need to think too hard about what might have come along to intervene.

"Savannah was gone by then. They had shipped her off to college. They wouldn't even tell me where. It was made quite clear that she had been sent away because of me. It seemed our meetings weren't quite as secret as we thought they were. I went back to the carnival, deciding that was to be my life. If I couldn't have her, what was the point?" His eyes came back to meet Penelope's, filled with defiance. "I know I sound like some love-struck puppy who went after steak when all I deserved was scraps."

"Of course I don't think that," Pen protested, wondering why he would assume that of her.

"Well, that's exactly what they thought, and I couldn't help feeling the same at the time," he said bitterly. "If it wasn't for my mother deciding I needed a rescue, I'd probably still be in that carnival. She remembered Agnes, how passionate she'd been about art, and so she brought me up here to New York and," his mouth hitched up into a half smile, "I guess she saw something in me. Or maybe just took pity on me. Next thing I knew, I was on some swanky ship to France."

"How did you learn Savannah was here in Long Island?"

"Bruce Carlton," he said with a hard edge to his voice.

There was a name familiar to Penelope. The Carltons were one of the families in the same circles among which she had grown up. Bruce, in particular, had never been a favorite of hers. In fact, she remembered him being quite the bully growing up. He, of course, never bothered Penelope after the one time he dared drop a handful of worms down the back of her dress. Instead of falling to the ground like the squealing damsel in distress he'd expected, she had chased him down and tackled him to the ground. She had then grabbed a fistful of dirt to rub into his mouth, even as all of those creepy crawlers slithered across her back.

Pen instinctively arched her back at the slimy memory of it. It had been worth it just for the utter look of shock and humiliation on Bruce's face. By all accounts, he'd grown up into the same type of bully as an adult. Pen had heard mutterings about his arrogant snobbery and jealous nature, among his other vices.

"Don't tell me she's involved with *him*?" Penelope asked with dismay.

James tilted his head and considered her, his jaw hardening as he answered. "She's engaged to him is what she is, they officially announced just before I arrived."

Pen didn't bother with society pages anymore. Engagements, weddings, and other such announcements no longer interested her the way they once had, so this was new information.

"I see," Penelope said. She decided to set aside the issue of an engaged woman coming to visit James at his cottage. Instead, her brow furrowed in confusion.

"How did you find out about the engagement in Paris if it hadn't even been announced yet?"

He inhaled, as though that too was a long story. "When Agnes first sent me to Paris, I immersed myself in my life there, trying to forget about Savannah. My mother was the one to tell Savannah that I was in Paris. Maybe she really did have the eye," James said with a wry smile. "I had been in France almost two years when I got her first letter. We wrote to each other constantly. She even came to visit me at one point. Those were the happiest two weeks of my life."

He paused to look off to the side again as though remembering it.

"Then, about six months ago, her letters stopped coming. I still don't know why. Ultimately, it didn't really matter; she was gone. So, I fell back into the world of art again, trying to forget her. Then, about a month ago, I got a letter from her telling me the news of her upcoming engagement. I wasn't going to give her up without a fight. Not even now that the announcement has finally been made."

"What did she say when you finally met with her?"

He worked his jaw to the side in a guilty but rakish way. "Mostly, we just picked up where we left off from those two weeks in Paris. Though I have been painting her as well."

"I see," Pen said, leaving that suggestion alone. She wondered if "painting" was a euphemism.

"She doesn't love him," James insisted, his gaze darkening. "That first visit proved it. I can't for the life of me figure out why she's going through with the marriage."

"She is?" Penelope couldn't imagine any woman being daft enough to *want* to marry someone like Bruce.

"Yes, but I intend to win her back long before that."

"Do you have a plan this time?" Pen asked with a lighthearted smile.

It was enough to temper some of his intensity, and he exhaled a laugh. He considered her for a moment. "You know the Carltons, don't you?"

"Yes," she said warily.

"Perhaps you could invite them to tea or coffee or something like that?"

Penelope laughed, then instantly felt bad at his disheartened expression.

"I'm sorry, I wasn't laughing at you. It's just...if you knew my history with Bruce, you would know I'm not exactly someone likely to invite him to anything, let alone tea."

"But you're both in the same circles aren't you? I don't want to put you out, but surely if you asked, he'd be polite enough to take you up on it?"

"Polite is the last word I'd use to describe Bruce."

"I see," his face fell again, making him look younger and more pitiful.

Penelope studied him as she finished off her champagne. As loath as she was to ever see Bruce Carlton again, why not give Savannah a chance to change her mind? Better before the marriage than after. Pen knew that better than anyone.

"How about this, we'll invite ourselves to meet with them this afternoon."

His eyes brightened so much it nearly made Pen laugh. "Really?"

"Yes."

At the very least it would give James a better idea of what he was up against. The Carltons were quite wealthy. The homes in Sands Point may not have been as grandiose as those in Glen Cove, but they reeked of Old Money, the kind that wouldn't dwindle for generations, even in the hands of someone as useless as Bruce Carlton.

"Do you think they'll agree to meet with us?"

"I think Bruce wouldn't pass up the chance to gloat in front of me." At the curious expression on James's face, she explained. "I was once engaged and had to break it off. Also a long story. Infidelity."

A guilty look came to his face.

"Nothing like your situation—not exactly. I was under the impression we actually loved each other," Penelope said, a bitter twist to her mouth.

She was suddenly curious about this Savannah Duncan. Why was she going through with the marriage if she was still giving James this kind of hope? Was it the money? Was it some leverage Bruce had over her?

Now, Pen was almost as eager to have this meeting as James was.

CHAPTER FOUR

James had gone back to the cottage to change into something that befitted a more formal meeting.

While he did that, Penelope decided to inquire about him. First, she hunted down Chives. She found him in the staff area.

"Sorry to bother you, Chives, but I just had a question."

"Of course Miss Banks, how may I be of service?"

"It's about James Gaston, the man you saw me with just now."

"Ah," he said as though the question was expected.

"He said that Agnes was his sponsor and sent him to Paris to study art. That she also gave him an open invitation to stay at one of the cottages here. Have you ever seen him before? Granted, he says he's been away for the past five years, so it might have been some time ago."

Although Chives didn't have the same ability to remember everything like a photograph as she did, he did have a sharp mind that rarely forgot anything. He'd also been one of Agnes's most trusted employees.

"Yes, I recall briefly meeting him around that time."

This meant that at the very least, he wasn't an imposter posing as the real James Gaston.

Chives continued. "Though, I should say the interaction with Miss Sterling was all rather hushed and hurried."

"What do you mean?"

"That there were meetings I wasn't privy to. And the period between my introduction to Mr. Gaston and his leaving for Paris was quite brief."

"As though Agnes didn't want anyone to know about him?"

"I couldn't say, Miss."

"Did she happen to tell you anything about him?"

"No, Miss Banks."

Penelope gave him a coy look before pressing him even more. "Did you happen to *overhear* anything about him?"

"No, Miss Banks," he said just as diplomatically.

Of course he would be discreet about anything he had inadvertently learned, even well after Agnes's death. Pen should have been grateful that he'd likely be just as tight-lipped should something unfortunate happen to her. For now, it was rather frustrating.

"I see, well thank you, Chives."

She left him and went to find the phone to call Mr. Wilcox. He had been the one to handle these things for Agnes, so perhaps he could be more informative and less discreet.

Once she was connected, she was immediately put through to him. As Agnes's main beneficiary, Pen was now an important client of his, so she received preferential treatment.

"Miss Banks, how is it I can help you?" He answered in a warm tone.

"I'm calling about one of the artists Agnes may have sponsored, a James Gaston. Does the name sound familiar?"

"James Gaston..." he said thoughtfully. "I'll have to check my records."

"It would have been about five years ago. She sent him to Paris, quite promptly it would seem."

"Ah now, that does ring a bell. It deviated from how she usually handled those sorts of things, though Agnes was never one for predictability. Still, spending that much money to send him to Paris right away seemed rather odd."

"Do you think she may have wanted to keep him hidden away for some reason?"

"If she did she certainly didn't confide in me. Though, I should state, an allowance left for him was included in the various trusts and endowments she set up outside of her will. It isn't much, mind you, just enough to support a young artist in a small apartment in Paris."

"Even after her death?"

"Oh yes."

"He couldn't be...her son, could he? One she maybe gave up for adoption?"

Mr. Wilcox laughed. "When it came to Agnes, one never knew. Still, I suspect if he had been, she would have been more generous with him, specifically with regard to her will, don't you think?"

He did have a point. Penelope had inherited the lion's share of Agnes's estate. Thus, unless James had done something to earn her disfavor, it surely would have been left to him if he were her secret son. Besides, James didn't at all resemble Agnes. Then again, perhaps he took mostly after his father? Penelope took entirely after her mother, save for the bright blue eyes she'd inherited from her father. Of course, Pen's were far more vivacious and even slightly mischievous in the way her mother's green eyes had been.

"Miss Sterling was a very peculiar woman, Miss Banks. And I say that in the most complimentary way. All the same, whatever her relationship with this young man, I wasn't privy to it. I simply followed orders. I could check my records to give you the exact details regarding amounts and whatnot."

"No, thank you, I just wanted to make sure he was who he said he was."

"Well, if he says he is an artist by the name of James Gaston, who Agnes sponsored and sent to study art in Paris, then yes he is."

"And you don't know anything else about him?"

"Agnes told me what she wanted to tell me about these little artistic generosities of hers, and that wasn't much. I did my due diligence to make sure that they were on the up and up, after that she took the reins."

"And what did your due diligence tell you about this fellow?"

"That's the odd thing, Miss Sterling insisted that I leave it alone, that she had good reason to trust him and his abilities. In fact, I got the impression she didn't want me to investigate him at all. Which of course made me all the more suspicious. Still, even if I had wanted to look into him, I didn't even have so much as a city of birth to start with. I certainly wasn't going to bother hiring someone to look into him against her wishes."

If James really had grown up in a carnival, it would have been near impossible to learn anything official about him. There might not even be a record of his birth. Many rural families simply documented new additions in the family Bible and left it at that. Pen wondered if there was even that much of a record for James.

"Thank you, Mr. Wilcox."

"Has Mr. Gaston returned to New York then?"

"He's been staying in the cottage here on the property. He claims Agnes gave him free use whenever he returned."

"That is something I don't know anything about, perhaps it was an informal agreement between them. Of course, as one of the legal tenants of the property for the next several months, you're entitled to have him ejected."

"That's not necessary. I don't consider him a threat and, knowing Agnes, she may very well have extended him that sort of informal invitation. I certainly don't want to defy her wishes. At least not until I have a good reason to."

"I can have someone look into him if you like."

"What kind of private investigator would I be if I asked that of you?" she said smartly, though not without some good humor.

"Ah yes, forgive my slight," he said with a chuckle. "By now, I should have more faith in your investigative abilities, Miss Banks."

"Thank you for taking the time to speak with me, Mr. Wilcox."

"Of course Miss Banks, and don't hesitate to call if you need anything else."

"Thank you, good day."

"Good day."

Penelope hung up and thought about everything she learned from Chives and Mr. Wilcox. It was obvious Agnes was keeping James a secret from everyone, including the two people who should have been the most informed. The question was, why?

CHAPTER FIVE

"Well you certainly clean up nicely," Pen said when James reappeared after changing. He now wore a nice suit, lightweight material in a soft cream color. He'd combed his hair back into something respectable, though it still curled over his collar in the back. Pen had to admit, he did look rather debonaire, even in the middle of the afternoon.

Fortunately, Penelope had prepared for her birthday week in Long Island and brought only her best dresses. She had changed into a sky blue slip dress with a white lace overdress, paired with matching shoes and a hat.

Leonard was waiting with the Rolls Royce Silver Ghost to drive them around the bay to Sands Point. At the very least, they arrived in high style.

The Carlton home was done in a Tudor style made out of gray stone, probably meant to look like a British castle. Penelope had always thought it looked more like a prison, at least from the front. The small transom windows above the larger picture windows had diamond-patterned stained glass in varying shades of green. It was the only hint of color on an otherwise dreary facade.

Leonard opened the car door for them and she led James up the steps and rang the doorbell. Penelope hadn't sent a calling card or any notice of that kind, and it was rather rude to simply drop in on someone who wasn't a friend or even an acquaintance. In fact, she wouldn't have put it past Bruce to turn them away just for the embarrassment of it.

The front doors were opened by a butler who greeted them cordially enough. She gave their names, informing him that they were there to meet with Bruce Carlton and Savannah Duncan. He left them in the grand foyer, with marble flooring and a large cut glass chandelier above, while he inquired further within.

If James was at all intimidated by the trappings of wealth around him he didn't show it. In fact, his eyes were fixed upon the archway through which the butler had disappeared. When he returned, the intensity in James's gaze only deepened.

"I'm afraid Mr. Carlton is unavailable at the moment." Pen was disappointed, but not surprised. It was summer in Long Island after all. He could have been up to a number of activities or visiting with friends. "However, Miss Duncan will see you in the solarium."

That brightened both their hopes and they followed the butler further in. When they passed by the sitting room, Penelope was forced to momentarily stop when James paused next to her. She followed his gaze to a picture hanging on one wall in that room. It was of a young, blonde woman, done in pastel colors and soft brushstrokes, giving her an ethereal appearance. She was sitting on a blanket on a rooftop in what was obviously Paris, based on the architecture in the background. Unlike with most portraits, she looked directly at the painter with a hint of a smile on her lips. It showed promise in the artist, even though it was quite obvious he was copying some of the greats, as many new artists did before finding their own style. In fact, it rather reminded Penelope of a Degas painting.

So, this was the mysterious Savannah Duncan.

Noting that Penelope was studying the painting, James quickly continued on. She couldn't tell if he was embarrassed by the work, or if it had just made him more eager to see the real-life subject of the piece.

In the solarium, all the French doors, which faced the stately pool and beyond that, Long Island Sound, were open to allow the sea breeze to enter. There were electric fans above, spinning at a lackadaisical pace that matched the languor of the first woman upon which Pen's eyes landed. She was draped across a chaise lounge, dressed in black, wearing sunglasses, and smoking a cigarette in a holder. More noteworthy, shocking even, she wore a pair of long, wide-leg trousers.

"Savannah," James whispered next to Pen, his attention set in an entirely different direction.

Penelope tore her eyes away from that first woman, who still hadn't acknowledged their arrival, and shifted them to the figure with her back to them as she continued to stare out the windows.

"Now then, that's an awfully familiar greeting." This came from the woman in the chaise lounge who suddenly swung her legs to the side to sit up and face them. She lifted her glasses so they were perched atop her brunette Eton crop haircut, and studied the two arrivals as she took a long drag on her cigarette in its holder.

"Miss Duncan, I meant to say," James said before clearing his throat, his eyes still firmly planted on the woman before them.

Despite how interesting the woman sitting on the chaise lounge was, Penelope once again dragged her eyes away to stare at the woman staring out the window. Her long, white-blonde hair was pulled into a chignon at the back of her neck. She had a slight, but feminine figure draped in white almost down to her ankles.

Savannah slowly turned around, as though facing a ghost she had thus far been afraid to confront. Penelope imagined that face looking up from a book on Degas, and could see how a seventeen-year-old boy would have instantly fallen for her. Savannah was pretty in a way that probably made men feel more manly by comparison, with delicate features, wide blue eyes, and a heart-shaped face.

Savannah stared at James as though under a spell. Her lips parted to silently utter something Pen was certain was his name. She blinked twice and her eyes flitted to Penelope standing beside him. There was a flicker of something Pen couldn't quite read, but it wasn't anything amicable.

"You must be Savannah Duncan," Pen greeted in a pleasant tone. "I'm Penelope Banks, staying across the bay in Glen Cove. This is James Gaston, a *friend* staying with me this weekend." She made sure to stress the word friend. The last thing she wanted was to become the fourth corner in this mess of a love triangle. She had also made sure to introduce him as though they were all strangers, just in case.

"It's...very nice to meet you, Miss Banks," Savannah said, a faltering smile coming to her lips. She quickly added, "You as well, Mr. Gaston."

There was an appealing, soft lilt of a southern accent in her voice. Her eyes fell on James with a mix of trepidation and longing as she continued. "And what brings you here today?"

"I heard of your engagement. Bruce and I, well, we go

back a ways, and I wanted to come and congratulate him. And of course meet his lovely bride-to-be, with whom I have yet to be introduced." Penelope walked over and Savannah's eyes widened with alarm. "Congratulations."

"Thank you kindly," Savannah said with a more relaxed smile as she accepted Penelope's kiss on the cheek. Her eyes slid past Pen to the man still standing in the doorway. "And you, Mr. Gaston, have you come to offer your congratulations as well?"

Penelope turned to look at him. James's jaw tensed before he breathed out a terse, "Congratulations."

A chuckle emanated from the woman still smoking on the chaise lounge. "I could positively suffocate from how thick the tension in the room is right now."

Penelope turned to her with one eyebrow arched. "And who might you be?"

"Joan Dyson. The cousin. Carlton side. Actually, second cousin...or first cousin once removed. Second cousin twice removed?" Joan said with a shrug and a laugh. "Just call it distant enough that Brucie-boy easily dismisses me. I think the entire Carlton side would rather I didn't exist at all. Thus, I spend most of my time in Boston."

Joan tilted her head and studied Penelope with an ambiguous smile. She had dark but glittering eyes as though the entire world was a source of ironic amusement for her. "Penelope Banks. Now, how do I know that name?"

Penelope felt her back go rigid. She hoped that, despite being from Boston, Joan *wouldn't* recognize her name. Penelope's ex-fiancé, Clifford Stokes, had retreated back to that city after their failed, and quite scandalous engagement.

"Ah yes, a private detective, or so I've heard," Joan said. Still, there was something in her gaze that told Pen she knew all about Clifford, though she might just keep that to herself.

"Are you in Long Island to celebrate the engagement?" Pen asked, hoping to move away from the topic of Boston.

"Oh no, I model. Mostly in the ever-growing field of women's sportswear," she said, kicking up a trousered leg. "Really I have no home, I flit about from one city to another, whenever the mood takes me, and with whomever will have me. Fortunately, the mood has landed me in Long Island this summer. I have a feeling it's going to finish off rather *sultry*, don't you?" Her eyes darted back and forth between the two obvious lovebirds on either side of them.

"I wouldn't know," Penelope said tactfully. "I only came to offer my congratulations."

"Say, I've heard you're hosting *the* party of the summer this weekend and everyone is invited, *supposedly*." She gave an exaggerated pout as she turned to Savannah. "Did you get an invitation, Savie dear?"

Savannah dragged her eyes away from James. They landed on Joan with a hint of exasperation. "You'd have to ask Bruce, he handles all of that...for me."

That last bit hung in the air, heavy with meaning. Now Pen was even more curious as to her reason for marrying Bruce. She already seemed weighed down by the yoke of his control.

"Of course you're invited," Penelope quickly said. "All of you."

"How swell!" Joan sang. "But aren't we being such rude hostesses? Please, please, let's retreat inside to the sitting room and have drinks. This beating sun is wearing on me. Do tell me you're both lawbreakers."

"Naturally," Penelope said following her inside.

"Splendid!"

The windows to the sitting room were also open, looking out on the sound. Pen sat on a sofa facing the wall with the painting of Savannah so she could study it better. It was all the more fortuitous when the subject herself sat on the couch right in front of it, as though she was used to sitting in that spot. The sun had traveled far enough for its rays to hit the green stained glass of the transom windows. It gave the painting a strange emerald glow, making it seem sacred and untouchable.

James was wise enough to sit next to Pen. Or perhaps he also wanted to admire the view.

"Please tell me you take it straight up," Joan said, walking to the small bar with an array of bottles. "I'm no good at cocktails."

"Joan, it's still only afternoon," Savannah said with a sigh.

"The perfect time for whiskey then," she replied, grabbing a glass and pouring herself a good dose.

"I'll take gin," Penelope said, earning her a chuckle of camaraderie from Joan, who poured just as much of that into a new glass.

"Any other requests?"

"Nothing for me, thank you," James said, his gaze still on Savannah.

"Nor for me," Savannah added, lowering her eyes to her hands twisted in her lap.

Now that Penelope had a chance to study her, she could see Savannah came from good breeding. Her clothes were fine, but that didn't mean much. Bruce would have been the type of man to dress his fiancée to impress others. That also explained the ring on the finger of one hand, which she was taking pains to keep hidden underneath the other. Pen had already eyed the large sapphire surrounded by diamonds. It was almost gaudy in its grandeur.

Joan handed Pen her drink then walked over and fell onto the couch next to Savannah with her own in her hand. Her eyes danced from one person to the other, as though deciding which target to toy with first. Before she could commit that bit of mischief, they were interrupted by the sound of others arriving through a back door somewhere. One moment later Bruce Carlton and two other young men made an appearance.

"Well, well, well, it seems we have company, gentlemen," Bruce said, staring at Pen with a wicked gleam in his eye. "Pen, whatever brings you to this side of the bay?"

CHAPTER SIX

"I came to congratulate you on your engagement, Bruce," Penelope said as cordially as she could muster, ignoring the air of smugness coloring his expression.

From a strictly objective point of view, Bruce looked too proud to be considered handsome. His brow was too high, his nose too narrow, his lips too thin, yet pouty, as though he found fault with everyone around him. His dark blonde hair was combed straight back, creating a widow's peak. While a certain class did appreciate patrician features, there was such a thing as too much of it. Bruce always reminded Penelope of those caricatures cartoonists made of snobby, aristocratic people.

Compared to James, he presented an inferior picture even though he was tall and fit in a slender way. Just now, he sported the golden hue that came from having spent the morning on the water.

"Pen coming by to congratulate me? I would have thought you'd be put off by any talk of an *engagement*." He laughed at his own little bit of ribbing.

Penelope didn't deign to reply, knowing full well his only intent was to embarrass her.

It seemed she wasn't the only one barely able to keep their contempt in check. The only difference was that the man standing next to Bruce was staring at James instead, his expression filled with undisguised venom. The white blonde hair, fine features, and wide blue eyes exposed him as Savannah's brother. It was quite obvious that he knew who James was, and more importantly, his history with Savannah.

The young man on Bruce's other side had dark hair and sported the same bronze hue as Bruce (Savannah's brother had a rather unfortunate sunburn). Penelope recognized him as Morris Belmont. Apparently, he had decided to abandon his parents in Newport. Either he hadn't yet learned that his family's maid had been murdered or he didn't consider it news worthy of ruining his day out with Bruce.

Bruce's assessing eyes fell on James again. The competitive edge in his gaze told Pen he was mentally measuring himself against James and found himself wanting. "Are you Pen's new beau? Has she finally moved on from Clifford?" He asked with a chuckle.

"This is James Gaston, a *friend* staying with me here in Long Island in one of the cottages on the property."

Bruce seemed to find that even more amusing and he laughed as he went over to the bar to pour himself some whiskey. "How very convenient for you, Pen. These are modern times, after all."

She felt her cheeks burn at the suggestion.

"As Penelope stated, I'm just a friend, nothing more," James said curtly. "In fact, I'd say I have a much better view of *your* home from there."

There was a blatant message in his wording, though Pen was certain Bruce wouldn't appreciate it. Even if he did know about James's relationship with Savannah, he would be too thick-headed to appreciate it.

Morris on the other hand considered him with an intrigued look and a half-cocked smile on his lips. "Do a lot of sightseeing do you? I suppose you even have a pair of binoculars for a little, ah, birdwatching?"

James briefly directed his attention to Morris. "It's surprising what one sees that others fail to notice."

Everyone in the room by now realized there was a hidden note of meaning there, meant specifically for Bruce. Morris and Finn, in solidarity with Bruce, both narrowed their gazes at James. Bruce, however, seemed to be clueless about the subtle messages being bandied about, based on the way he twisted his lips to the side with consternation.

"So Penelope is still holding a flame for Clifford after all these years then?" Bruce turned to Savannah's brother with a smirk. "Our Pen was jilted at the altar, Finn."

"Wasn't he found with Constance Gilmore the night before the wedding?" Morris said as he joined Bruce at the bar to pour a drink for himself. "And *you* were the one to call off the wedding, weren't you, Pen? Can't say I blame you for that one."

Penelope sighed and sipped her gin, wondering how she could shift the discussion to a different topic.

"*Savannah*, may we speak in private," Finn gritted out in a southern drawl, glaring at his sister. Apparently, all the talk of infidelity was striking a nerve with him.

"I'm already settled, Finn. Perhaps later," Savannah said in a surprisingly defiant manner.

"*Savannah*," he urged.

"Now, now, Finn, if my future wife says she's fine then

she's fine. Besides, whatever you have to say to her you can say in front of me. After all, we're soon to be family, no need for secrets."

Penelope couldn't help feeling a wee bit amused at the idea that Bruce had no idea what was going on right underneath his nose. From the look on Joan's face, she felt the same way, though she did a much worse job of masking her enjoyment.

"Let's all sit and get acquainted with one another. After all, it's been so long since I've visited with you, Pen," Bruce said, taking a seat on the armchair that offered a view of the entire room.

"I believe you had a mouthful of dirt last time we *visited*, so it would have been difficult to hold a conversation," she replied with a sweet smile. She couldn't help herself.

Bruce glared at her, but quickly snuffed it out and chuckled. "Ah yes, we did play our little pranks on each other, didn't we? But one grows out of those silly antics, and eventually settles down. Or at least some of us do. Have you shown Pen your ring yet, sweetheart?" he said to Savannah, his eyes still trained on Penelope.

"I've seen it. It was rather impossible to miss," Penelope said, still smiling graciously.

Joan snickered, which had Bruce's eyes narrowing as though wondering if he was the butt of a joke.

Finn, having given up his attempt to have a firm talk with his sister, stormed over to the bar and poured himself too much gin. Then, he joined Morris to settle into the second chair on the other side of the room from Bruce, which also offered a view of everyone else.

"Penelope has officially extended to all of us an invitation to her party this Saturday," Joan said. "Please tell me there will be a full jazz band and fireworks?"

"Naturally," Pen said, suddenly regretting the open invitation.

"Party?" Bruce said.

"Savannah and I have already agreed to go," Joan quickly said.

"Have you?" Bruce's hardened gaze shifted to Savannah, whose eyes remained idly on the floor before her.

"Yes, I think you should come with us," Joan continued. "It's going to be wicked fun."

"Look at our Pen, your own money to play with. We should all be so lucky," Morris said in a sardonic tone.

"Of course we'll go, since Pen has *personally* invited us," Bruce said. "It's twenty-five this year, isn't it? Next thing you know you'll be thirty. That's officially spinster territory."

Penelope could see that he was going to use her failed wedding as fodder the entire afternoon. She had a smart retort on the tip of her tongue but James intervened.

"Have you set a date for your wedding?" he asked, meeting Bruce with a level gaze.

"What concern is that of yours?" Finn snapped.

"Well, we *are* here to congratulate you on your engagement, after all," Pen answered. She turned to Bruce. "*Do* you have a date for the wedding?"

He chuckled. "We only just announced, Pen. Those details can be worked out with my mother and Savannah. My job is to show up at the altar, right sweetheart?" He lifted his glass and laughed. Savannah just stared down at her ring, her expression unreadable.

Pen was getting rather bored of all this talk of weddings. She didn't want to inadvertently reveal James or his plans, but she had a feeling that might just happen if they continued down this path. Instead, she brought up the only other bit of news she could think of, mostly because she had one of the Belmonts right there.

"I was sorry to hear about your family's maid, Morris."

"My maid?" he replied, a confused smile coming to his lips.

"Martha Combs. You didn't hear?"

He simply raised his brow expectantly.

"She was run over last night, on Brookline Drive over in Glen Cove. The police think it was deliberate."

"You don't say?" Morris said, blinking in surprise. "What the hell was she doing in Glen Cove, or Long Island for that matter?"

"So she wasn't meant to be at your home here?"

"Not since we left for Newport. Why would we keep a maid out here? She *should* have been back at the apartment in the city." He stared hard into his drink for a moment before taking a long sip. The only indication this news was upsetting to him was a furrowed brow, though it seemed more a reflection of being mildly annoyed rather than saddened or disturbed.

"My, my, Morris, what an unfortunate welcome to Long Island that must be for you," Joan said with sympathy that was too overt to be genuine. She was definitely hinting at something cryptic.

"Darren is sure to be broken up over this," Morris muttered, his brow furrowed in consternation.

"Darren?" Penelope asked.

He lifted his gaze. "Our chauffeur. Martha was his wife."

"One would have thought he'd have noted her being gone last night," Penelope said.

"He's still in Newport with my parents," Morris said distractedly. "Who the hell is going to be the one to tell him? He's dizzy for the girl, but then, who could blame him? He certainly did well for himself with her."

"Did *you* miss her at all last night, Morris?" Joan asked in a suggestive manner.

Morris snapped his attention to Joan, his eyes narrowed with irritation. "I wasn't even in Long Island last night, as you well know. I only returned this morning."

"They found her less than a mile from where I am. Any idea what she might have been doing over there?"

Morris gave Penelope a bewildered look. "What the hell do I know what our maid gets up to at night? Probably visiting one of the workmen or delivery boys for your upcoming party. It wouldn't be the first time she's skated around, I can tell you. *That's* where the police should put their focus, rather than questioning decent upstanding members of society."

"Oh, I don't know," Joan mused with an impish look, as though she were in on a secret. "So often you find decent, upstanding members of society becoming entangled with those who, *ahem*, service them."

"Perhaps it was you she was going to visit, Joan. We all know which part of the barnyard you lay your eggs."

"Why Morris, do stop, you're making our guests blush," Joan said, completely unbothered.

"Is that why my cufflinks keep going missing? If you're looking to impress the ladies, Joan, that isn't exactly the sort of, ah, equipment that will impress them." Bruce said with a taunting chuckle. Morris and Finn joined in.

Penelope found herself increasingly appalled at how cavalier they were being in the face of a murdered woman. Yes, the upper class had a tendency to ignore those settled in stations below them, but they should have shown at least a bit of somber appreciation when it came to death. Particularly if it was murder.

"Obviously she was meeting some egg over in Glen Cove. The lower classes are so easily impressed with the tastelessly grandiose mansions on that side of the bay. They have no appreciation for class and subtlety," Bruce said, sounding slightly defensive.

"Yes, class and subtlety are certainly the first words that come to mind when one thinks of your lovely home," Penelope said. Joan snickered again.

Bruce frowned at Pen, rapidly swirling his drink with displeasure. "Perhaps you've spent too much time among them during those years of debauchery in jazz clubs, Pen. Oh yes, we know all about your adventures playing cards with the seedy underbelly of society. The lower classes are low for a reason. It only makes sense that they would try to claw themselves up using any means available to them. Perhaps the Glen Cove set is more susceptible to flattery from a common maid, getting it on after nothing more than a dimpled smile, flaming hair, and a comely figure."

"I had forgotten how enlightened your views on society were," Penelope said in a withering tone. "Your insight is truly something to behold."

"I read up on these matters a lot. There's plenty of interesting work out there if one wants to educate themselves on the betterment of society. A firm separation of the classes is important."

"But you've obviously crossed those lines at some point. Your description of Mrs. Combs is quite accurate," Pen said, giving him a questioning look.

"Morris and I are pals, Pen. Of course I would have noticed a tomato like her while visiting him."

"Really, Bruce," Savannah scolded with a frown. "Have we forgotten that she's been murdered?"

"Yes, yes, yes, may she rest in peace, and all that jazz," Bruce muttered, lifting his glass by way of apology. "I hadn't forgotten."

His brow arched and he gave Penelope a considering look. "But again, she was caught in your neck of the woods, wasn't she, Pen? Which I suppose points the finger at you, or perhaps someone staying with you?" He kept his eyes on her, but it was obvious he was referring to James.

"One does wonder how she got all the way over there in the first place, though. I don't suppose she had her own mode of transportation?" Pen directed the question to Morris.

"How would I know? The damn woman was *supposed* to be in Manhattan," he snapped. "Besides, as I said, I wasn't even here last night. Bruce will tell you, he saw me drive in just this morning."

"Absolutely," Bruce asserted. "Which I suppose puts the ball back on your side of the net, Pen. When did you and your *friend* arrive?"

"Just this week," she said idly.

"Seems awfully suspicious."

"Oh stop, Bruce, you've teased her enough," Joan said in a bored tone.

Throughout the entire interaction, Penelope had noticed that James and Savannah couldn't help casting surreptitious glances at one another, despite the macabre topic. Finn had certainly been aware of it as well, based on his sour expression. She wondered how long it would take Bruce to notice.

Not long, as it turned out.

"I don't think I'm quite familiar with any *Gaston* family.

What is it you do, James?" Bruce asked, his hard gaze studying the man.

"I'm an artist," he responded without embarrassment or apology. Bruce and Morris laughed in response. Finn coughed out a sharper, harsher laugh. James met it all with nothing more than a steady gaze.

Something seemed to suddenly click in place for Bruce, and his eyes slid up to the painting on the wall just above his fiancée. His gaze sharpened into daggers, as though slashing through the canvas from a distance.

"I see," he muttered. He slid his eyes to Penelope, giving her the same hateful look he'd sported when she'd repaid him for the worms down her back. "I think maybe you and your *friend* have just about overstayed your welcome, Pen. Savannah and I...have things to attend to."

"Yes, I suppose so," Pen said, offering the same cordial smile she'd forced to her lips during the entire visit.

She rose and caught James's eye. He seemed reluctant to tear his gaze away from Savannah, but stood and gave a slight nod to everyone in the room.

"I look forward to seeing you all this weekend," James said.

"As do I," Bruce said in a quietly sullen manner, swirling the contents of his glass around as he met James with narrowed eyes. "As do I."

CHAPTER SEVEN

"I'm afraid the jig is up, boy-o," Penelope said as James and she exited the Carlton home.

"It was inevitable that he would find out at some point," James said staring ahead. Penelope didn't miss the subtle smile gracing his lips.

"You *wanted* to confront him, didn't you?" she accused, as Leonard opened the door for them.

"No, not really. I mostly wanted to see who my competition was. Still, it's better that he knows sooner rather than later. When I win Savannah back, and I will, I'd rather do it fairly rather than behind his back."

"They do say *all* is fair in love and war."

"Then may the best man win," James said, now with a fully formed grin as he settled in the back seat next to her.

"Be forewarned, I know firsthand that Bruce is a sore loser." He'd gone crying to the adults after she'd smeared dirt in his face, accusing her of being the instigator. Pen hadn't exactly had the most saintly reputation as a child, which was enough to find him credulous, and she'd been punished accordingly.

James shook his head with a firm set to his mouth. "I waited five years for her, I'm not giving up that easily."

It did appear the engagement was rather settled. Also, Savannah's brother didn't seem very happy to see James. The Carltons had a lot of money. That only led to the obvious conclusion, that the Duncans needed the Carlton wealth.

Families like the Carltons took marriage seriously. Not with any sentimental or religious regard, but in the far more imposing matter of status. Suffering the embarrassment of a broken engagement wasn't something they'd react to lightly.

Penelope kept all of this to herself.

"I take it that was your painting in the sitting room?"

"Some of my earlier work," he said with an amused grimace. "I've improved since then."

"It wasn't terrible."

"No, it's not a good representation of my development."

"There's emotion in it that anyone can see, and not only from the artist. The way she stares back, I understand why she held onto it."

Penelope realized that they had turned onto Brookline Drive, where Martha had been killed. She focused her attention on the road ahead wondering where it had happened. They passed the gates and drives that led to the homes settled more inland in Glen Cove. They became less and less frequent until they reached an area that was still wild and empty, nothing but brush, trees, and grass.

"Stop, Leonard!"

He came to a screeching halt, tires squealing against the road. He swiveled around and gave her a look that was a mixture of exasperation and alarm. "Something wrong, Miss Banks?"

"Sorry, I just need to check something. Wait here a moment."

Pen opened the door for herself and got out. She walked back towards the dark patch on the road she'd seen. She stared down at it, feeling the sorrow and revulsion overcome her as she recognized what it was. She imagined being out here in the middle of the night with nothing more than some mad man, or woman, intent on running her down. Martha must have been terrified.

Pen heard Leonard and James exiting the car. As she lifted her gaze to them, she noted the tire marks from where Leonard had skidded to a stop. Penelope dragged her eyes back to the scene of the crime. There were no tire marks there, which meant whoever had hit Martha hadn't even bothered using the brakes. No wonder the police thought it was murder. In fact, they said she had shown evidence of being run over more than once. Such a brutal way to go. Someone definitely wanted Martha dead.

But why?

Penelope could certainly think of a number of ways a maid could get someone into trouble. They knew everything that happened in the house. And Joan had been correct with her insinuation that some of them did find themselves "entangled" with members of the household they worked for, entangled in a way that could lead to even more trouble. Morris had even suggested she wasn't faithful.

"You find any clues?" Leonard asked. He'd worked with her on a few cases and knew she had a knack for figuring things out. Eventually.

"Does anything stand out for either of you? Why would Martha be on the road here of all places?"

"Well, this stretch of the road is pretty isolated," Leonard said. "There's nothing around here."

"Maybe that was the point. No one to hear anything."

They stood there absorbing that fact.

"All right, I suppose we should go," Pen finally said with a sigh when nothing else came to her. The three of them walked back to the car.

As Leonard opened the door for her, her eyes landed on something in the grass next to where he'd come to a stop. Instead of getting in, she walked over to see what it was.

"Now, how did you get here?" she muttered to herself, staring down at a pink jellybean.

She inspected the area around it and noticed the subtle signs of someone having gone through it. Nothing that would have caught the eye of a police officer, especially late at night. Still, this wasn't the kind of road one simply strolled along. There were no sidewalks or even natural paths for someone on foot to go by. Also, after more than a day or so, some animal would have come along to steal something sweet like this. Thus, it was likely to have come from Martha or the person who had killed her.

Penelope measured the distance from where Martha had been killed to this spot and it was a good ten or so yards. So how had she gotten from there to the middle of the road further down heading back toward Sands Point? Maybe the bit of candy wasn't related to Martha's death at all?

Pen debated picking it up or leaving it. If she left it, some animal might still come and abscond with it. On the other hand, taking it might interfere with any investigation. It was a shame they didn't make cameras more portable so a person could simply carry one around with them in a purse or a pocket.

"I want you two to be my witnesses. Note the pink jellybean here?" Pen said, pointing down to it.

The two of them crowded next to her, both staring down at the pink candy.

"Do you think this is related to her death?" Leonard asked.

"It seems a bit tenuous don't you think?" James said. He swiveled his head in the direction of the stain on the road. "It's pretty far away. I mean, the jellybean could have come from anyone. Even I took this road to get to the shore you see through the trees there."

"I suspect you're an exception to the rule, James. I don't think that's a very common means of getting to homes in this part of Glen Cove."

"Still, wouldn't the police have taken it if it was evidence?"

"They probably missed it. I'll just call and inform them about it. You two will back up my claim just in case they actually investigate it," Pen said, heading back to the car.

"It seems silly to call the police about something so minor, it's a piece of candy. Do you really want to hassle them so close to the date of your party? There's a lot of alcohol you have at the house," James said as he got into the back seat next to her.

"Why James, you sound awfully defensive," Penelope teased. "Are you a candy hoarder?"

James looked stricken, and Penelope felt bad about the little jibe. It was easy enough for someone in her position to make light of interacting with the police. He'd probably had a far different experience with law enforcement when he was in the carnival.

"I'm only teasing you," she said. "Not to worry. The police won't bother with my alcohol. They'd have to arrest all of Glen Cove! In fact, they may appreciate my informing them about this little clue."

He gave her an uncertain smile. "Of course."

When they arrived back at the house, Pen stopped James before he retreated to his cottage. "My friends are arriving this evening to stay here until the party on Saturday. Why don't you join us tonight for dinner out on the terrace around eight?"

"Thank you, I look forward to it," James said with a smile.

"Perfect! You can dazzle them with some of your famous French 75s. I'll have plenty of bottles of champagne waiting on ice."

Penelope was set to be on her way, but there was something troubling in his gaze as it lingered on her. It hinted that he had something important to tell her. "What is it?"

For a long moment, he just stared, conflict coloring his eyes.

"If it's about Savannah, I'm not judging, James. She hasn't taken her vows yet, after all."

"It's not that. It's just that I—I hadn't realized it was your birthday this week before I arrived."

"You had no reason to know before now."

His brow furrowed as though she'd said something to upset him. "Yes, I suppose so."

"If you'd also like a *personal* invitation to the party, yes, James, you're invited," she said with a small laugh.

He laughed, relaxing as though whatever was on his mind, he'd decided to let go of it. "Well thank you. I'll make sure to have my glad rags ready. I'll see you tonight, Penelope."

"Pen. It's what all my friends call me."

Something flashed in his eyes, but it quickly passed. "Pen it is then."

THE GREAT GASTON MURDER

Penelope left to head back to the mansion to call the police.

"Glen Cove Police Department," a man answered.

"Hello, this is Penelope Banks. I spoke with an officer this morning about Martha Combs's death?"

"Yes ma'am," he said, his voice suddenly showing more interest. "Do you have any information about the incident?"

"Yes, I was driving along Brookline Drive, or rather my driver was, and I happened to see a pink jellybean in the brush by the side of the road nearby."

There was a pause before he answered. "A pink jellybean?"

"Yes, sir, I thought it might be related to the case."

"Did you now? And how close to the scene of the crime was this jellybean?" He didn't bother hiding his skepticism.

"Well, it was about ten yards away, but still, I thought it might be important."

"So let me make sure I have this straight. You were tootling along the road in your car and you just happened to see a jellybean—"

"A pink one, yes."

"—not anywhere near the scene, but a full ten yards away?"

"Yes," she said curtly, feeling her irritation set in. She could already tell he was going to dismiss it as nothing. It made her all the more eager for him to take it seriously. "I would think that you would want every bit of information that might be related to the *crime*, no matter how seemingly insignificant, no?" She had made sure to stress the word "crime."

"Yes ma'am, I'll be sure to pass this very important information along."

"You do that," Penelope said, hanging up in a huff.

She'd forgotten how pig-headed some men could be. Perhaps he had been an officer who remembered her from Agnes Sterling's murder. Or perhaps he just thought the idea of a jellybean being the clue that solved that case was ridiculous.

Either way, Pen had performed her civic duty. She was ready to put this unfortunate business aside to prepare for seeing her friends tonight, and more importantly Richard Prescott, with whom she had become quite close these past several weeks.

CHAPTER EIGHT

"Happy Birthday!"

Penelope raced down the front steps of the mansion to greet the people spilling out of the first car to arrive tonight. Leonard was driving in Benjamin "Benny" Davenport, Lucille "Lulu" Simmons, and Jane Pugley, her associate at her private investigative business.

"I have far too much champagne on ice, or whatever else you fancy, and dinner will be set up on the back terrace. Chives will show each of you to your rooms, so go and get settled and I'll meet you in the back. We have a surprise guest," Pen said, grinning and waggling her eyebrows.

"Please tell me it's Rudolph Valentino wrapped in a bow," Benny crooned.

"If it was, do you think Pen would be stupid enough to share him, honey?" Lulu said, playfully slapping him on the shoulder.

"*Is* it a movie star?" Jane asked her eyes wide.

"No, but I've been assured a few famous faces may make an appearance this Saturday. Now, hurry, hurry, the drinks will be waiting for you when you come back down," Pen said, shooing them along into the house, as she saw the second car come up the drive.

This one was driven by Richard Prescott, a detective in the New York police force. He was driving Pen's older Cousin Cordelia. Richard parked and got out, making sure to open the door for Cousin Cordelia first before greeting Penelope.

"I know the big day isn't until Saturday, but happy birthday, all the same, my dear," Cousin Cordelia said with a kiss on the cheek.

"Thank you, cousin," Pen said, repeating the same information about dinner and drinks on the terrace.

Penelope was set to rush into the arms of Richard, but he had already reached into the back of his car to pull out a large bouquet of roses for her.

"I know you said no presents, but I couldn't very well arrive empty-handed."

Penelope took hold of the armful of fat, fragrant roses. "I suppose I can forgive flowers from my *suitor*," she said in a voice that she noted was a few octaves higher.

"Never pooh-pooh flowers, Penelope dear. You'll miss them when they stop coming," her older Cousin Cordelia said. Chives returned to escort both of them in as well.

"Thank you, Chives, I am quite weary from the ride in," Cousin Cordelia said with a weary sigh as she was led away. "I do hate leaving Lady Di and the kittens for so long," she fretted about her white Persian cat, Lady Dinah, and her offspring, who were fairly past the stage of "kittens" by now.

Richard lingered for a moment until they were gone, then he pulled Penelope in closer, the flowers pressed between them. She took a moment to admire his handsome face. His dark eyes were fringed by thick lashes and his dark hair was combed straight back underneath the hat he had yet to remove. Really, the man could give Gary Cooper some stiff competition in terms of appearance. The only thing most people might have seen as a flaw was the burn scar that ran from the bottom of his right ear over his lower jaw and down his neck, a souvenir of the Great War. After learning of the heroic way he had earned it, Penelope thought it made him even more attractive.

"Drinks on the terrace, hmm?"

"Yes, and don't start in on that, you'll give poor Cousin Cordelia an attack of the nerves."

He laughed, used to her cousin's constant fretting.

"Speaking of which, do you remember how you promised to take off your detective cap this weekend?"

"Yes," he said hesitantly, his smile fading.

"Well, you already know there will be enough champagne and other poison to ossify Long Island Sound itself."

"I'm not sure I remember it put quite that way, but go on."

"Yes, well, the party may get a bit outrageous, nothing illegal, just a fair lack of inhibition, let's say."

He sighed with resignation. "I assumed so. I have heard of Agnes's infamous parties and I expect you'll be following in her footsteps."

"You don't have to make it sound so daunting. You could perhaps relax and have a bit of fun while you're being so sinful."

"Sinful? I like the sound of that," he said, his grin reappearing as he pulled her in even closer.

"Richard! You'll ruin my pretty flowers."

"It's worth it," he said, reaching his other hand up to cup the back of her neck and draw her in for a kiss. Penelope savored it the way she had each one since that very first they'd shared on the rooftop of a building during a case almost a month ago. This was certainly something she could get *very* used to. The sound of the staff coming out to bring in everyone's luggage finally had them pulling apart.

Penelope idly tucked an imaginary hair behind her ear, as she always did when Richard caused butterflies in her stomach. And his kisses always had that effect on her. She walked him inside, his arm still around her until he pulled away to get refreshed in his room upstairs.

Since there were so many people spending the night, Penelope had been forced to take Agnes's old room that had been added on to the home on the first floor after the accident that had left her wheelchair-bound. Pen still considered it "Agnes's room," and tried to forget the morbid reminder that it was where her body had been found.

Penelope left the roses with Chives to put in a vase. She wandered out onto the terrace. Even though it was just an intimate grouping of friends and family, she saw no reason not to be festive. Her peacock blue silk dress shimmered under the chandelier in the foyer. Black fringe tickled her legs just below the knees as she walked. On her head, she wore a beaded band with a Peacock feather sticking up from the side, the lucky one she had often worn to the Peacock Club, where she'd once upon a time made a living playing cards.

Outside, a table had already been set up, covered in a white tablecloth with place settings for seven. There were enough candles to give them light, since the moon wouldn't be making an appearance if the thick layer of clouds was any indication. Hopefully, that wouldn't mean rain on the day of her party. All the same, she wouldn't let something as silly as nasty weather get her down. Pen smiled at the setting, feeling the excitement begin to fill her veins.

"I see they brought all the ingredients for a French 75."

Penelope turned at the sound of James's voice behind her. He was approaching the small bar to the side where Penelope had instructed Chives to place all the ingredients she remembered from the drink he'd made earlier today.

"My friends are upstairs changing right now. I hope you don't mind putting on a show for them. You're quite the talented tender of drinks."

"It wouldn't be the first time that I sang for my dinner," he said with a grin.

Penelope laughed. "Don't worry, you don't have to be on your best behavior with this lot. In fact, I insist that you aren't."

They heard the sound of her friends exiting through the French doors onto the terrace and Pen turned to greet Lulu and Jane, who were arm in arm on either side of Benny.

"You must be Miss Banks's mystery guest for the evening," Jane greeted with a smile.

"Why Pen, you shouldn't have," Benny said, eyeing James appreciatively.

"And just how is it you know our Pen?" Lulu asked giving him a cool assessing look. Lulu was a jazz singer at the Peacock Club of questionable ownership. It was only natural she would be less quick to warm up to anyone new.

James took it all with good grace. Having lived in Paris for the last five years, especially as an artist, he had no doubt been introduced to a wide variety of people. Thus, he didn't bat an eye at either Lulu's race or the way Benny practically devoured him with his eyes.

"Pen and I are..." he turned to Penelope and winked. "Co-conspirators."

"And here I thought I was your only partner in crime," Lulu said, casting a wry smile Pen's way.

"Careful, Detective Prescott will be out at any moment," Benny teased.

"You have a detective coming?" James asked with a quirked eyebrow and tilted his head toward the bar. "I hope we won't get into trouble."

"This weekend we are all criminals. Richard's never been all that fond of Prohibition anyway, thinks it's caused more problems than it solved. I firmly agree. *Detective Prescott* has assured me he's left his handcuffs back in Manhattan."

"A shame," Benny said under his breath. Lulu gave him a nudge, biting back a smile.

"I think I heard the word criminals," Richard announced, walking through the open French doors, looking like a movie star as he joined them.

"Come to join us in the den of iniquity, have you?" Benny teased.

"Well, when you put it that way," Richard said good-humoredly.

"I was just about to introduce everyone," Penelope said. "Richard, this is James Gaston."

"Detective Richard Prescott," he said, reaching a hand toward James. It was impossible to miss the fact that he had added "detective" in front of his name.

"Nice to meet you, detective," James said with an unbothered smile as he shook his hand.

Penelope studied Richard, who was studying James. At first, she thought it was indeed jealousy that had his eyes piercing the man so hard. But there was a concentration in his gaze that smacked of him putting on his detective hat, despite his earlier reassurances. He seemed to realize Pen was watching him and he forced a smile to his face as he finished shaking hands and letting go.

"I suppose the only other person that you haven't been introduced to is Lucille Simmons. You might remember her help in our first case together. She's a jazz singer."

"At the Peacock Club," Richard said with a wry grin.

"You can call me Lulu," her friend purred as she hung one hand in the air.

Richard bent over to kiss the back of her hand as though she were an aristocrat. That eased any lingering tension in the air.

"I do hope I'm not interrupting," Cousin Cordelia said as she made an appearance. Her eyes blinked a few times as they landed on Lulu. Penelope had warned her that this weekend would be an interesting mix of people. "My, we certainly are a, er, colorful group."

"Don't worry, you'll be smitten after a few drinks," Lulu teased with an unconcerned smirk. "Everyone else is."

"Don't be silly. Penelope's mother invited every flavor of individual to her infamous dinners. I'm *quite* continental myself, I'll have you know," Cousin Cordelia sniffed.

Pen bit back a smile and finished the introductions between those who didn't know each other. She explained that James was one of the artists Agnes had supported, who had just returned from Paris.

"And tonight, James is going to bring a bit of Paris here to us by making French 75s."

"All the better to curry favor with everyone," James said. "Though I do have a confession to make, the drink isn't necessarily French. I picked it up from an American who introduced me to this version of it while in Paris."

He went to work making the drinks while they chatted, mostly about the upcoming party. Once they all had their drinks, Benny was the first to raise a toast. "To Pen, who has certainly made this one of the more interesting years of my life."

"Chin, chin!" everyone agreed.

"To Pen, still one of the best card players I've ever met. One of these days we're going to have to get you back into that," Lulu added.

"Chin, chin!"

"To Miss Banks, the best boss I've ever had," Jane said.

"Oh no, honey," Lulu chided. "There will be no 'Miss Banks' tonight. We've got to get you out of saying that."

"I agree, Jane. It's my birthday and my only wish is that you at least call me Penelope from now on, or better yet, Pen."

"Penelope," Jane said hesitantly, as though her tongue was trying a new flavor. Pen knew from experience the drink in her hand would help that along nicely.

Rather than toast, Richard just cast a secret smile her way, which needed no interpretation. After months of ambiguity when she first knew him, he had finally made his feelings known to her. This weekend would hopefully cement their relationship.

"I suppose I should add my own toast," James said turning to Penelope with a smile. "To Penelope, who," he paused, studying her as though trying to find the right words, "is a firm reminder that...*friends* can be found under the most fortuitous circumstances."

"Chin, chin!" Penelope said, lifting her glass to him.

The first course was served and they all sat down to eat. Throughout dinner and dessert, James regaled them with stories from his time in Paris.

"It's almost enough to make me want to get on a boat and visit," Lulu said.

"Paris has always been my dream," Jane said, looking starry-eyed. Penelope wasn't sure if it was from the one glass of wine she had in addition to the French 75 or the city itself.

"Yes, yes, you must all go," Penelope said, feeling rather ossified herself. "But only in the spring. The city of love must be appreciated in all its glory when everything is in bloom. In fact, I think for my next birthday, I'll spend it in Paris. Something to top this Saturday's party." She frowned in thought. "But of course that'll mean I'll have to celebrate it early so you can see the blossoms at their finest."

"I agree we must all go to Paris," Cousin Cordelia sang, her face flushed from all the wine she had imbibed "under duress." She teetered in her seat as a wistful look came to her face. "Harold and I had our honeymoon in Paris. Such a romantic city..." she swooned, nearly falling off her chair. Jane, thankfully, caught her in time.

"I think perhaps that is my cue to leave, dear," Cousin Cordelia said, looking horrified. "Happy Birthday, Penelope."

"Thank you Cousin," Penelope said.

Jane escorted her back inside.

"Speaking of birthdays," Lulu said, casting a smile Penelope's way, "I know you said no presents, but I got something for you anyway." Before Penelope could protest, Lulu was out of her seat and through the French doors.

She came back with a black enamel box and placed it on the table in front of Pen. There were beautiful Chinese dragons painted on the outside.

"Oh, what a lovely box. Is it for jewelry?" She gave Lulu

a quizzical look. Lulu knew Pen wasn't very interested in jewelry, so it seemed an odd choice of gifts.

"Open it," Lulu urged pushing it toward her with one finger.

Penelope grinned and lifted the lid, then gasped at what she saw inside. Her eyes flashed up to Lulu.

"You *didn't!*"

CHAPTER NINE

THE PEOPLE AROUND THE TABLE WERE STILL SHOWING varying degrees of shock and awe over Lulu's gift. Penelope picked up the gun from the black, enamel case. It *was* rather lovely, she had to admit. More like an accessory than a weapon. The shiny metal glimmered in the candlelight, but the most stunning feature was the grip inlaid with beautiful jade.

"Frankly you need it, Pen," Lulu said in response to Penelope's exclamation. "It almost matches mine, which as you know, has an ivory handle."

"Do you even know how to use one of those things?" Richard protested, his brow furrowed with disapproval.

"I can learn, and Lulu is right, I do need one," Pen argued.

"Dare I ask where this came from? Or rather, from whom?" He said arching a brow toward Lulu.

"Pen knows who," Lulu said with a smirk, then turned to her. "And Tommy Callahan says happy birthday as well."

"Really, Lulu!" Pen said with exasperation, more so from her friend revealing that fact than the fact itself.

Tommy Callahan was the right-hand man for Mr. Sweeney, one of the most notorious gangsters in New York and owner of the Peacock Club. Neither of them had any reason to wish Pen a happy birthday, certainly not without any strings attached. During her years playing cards, after her uncanny ability to suss out mischief had been discovered, she had often been invited to work for Mr. Sweeney, who would have been more than happy to use her peculiar memory for his own devices.

"I knew it!" Richard exclaimed. "There is no way I'm allowing Penelope to—"

"Allowing me to what?" Pen interjected, now reserving her ire for him.

"It's a dangerous weapon, which you just admitted you don't know how to use."

"I'm pretty sure I know how to aim and shoot," she said in a testy voice.

The others looked on with varying degrees of alarm and amusement. Jane had come back from delivering Cousin Cordelia to her room and blinked in surprise at both the uproar and the gun still in Pen's hand.

"Besides, it's not even loaded…." Pen turned to Lulu in alarm. "Is it?"

"Not yet, but the bullets are included. Check the little compartment on the side."

Penelope saw there was a little shelf that pulled out. She found six bullets inside. "Well, then, see? I'll just leave those safely in there."

Before Richard could protest further, they heard the sound of a boat hitting the dock. Everyone at the table turned to look toward the water. Via the lights from the mansion and the candles, they could just barely make out two figures as they stepped out and walked up the dock.

"Well, hello there," Joan greeted as she boldly ascended the stairs and approached them at the table.

She was wearing pants again, in a black silk pajama style with a red Chinese top and matching red moccasins. "Savannah and I saw there was a little party happening from across the bay. Confession, I snooped you all through Bruce's telescope. I'm nothing if not a shameless Nosey Nellie. We thought we'd ship ourselves over uninvited. That does seem to be the theme of the day." She gave Penelope a knowing wink.

Savannah, again dressed in a modest white dress, only had eyes for one person at the table. James was already out of his seat to meet her. The only thing that could tear their gazes away was Joan exclaiming at Penelope's gift.

"My God, is that what I think it is!"

Penelope instantly placed the gift Lulu had given her back into the enamel box and slammed shut the lid.

"Oh, no you don't," Joan said, rushing over to the other side of the table. She took hold of the sides of the box to turn it towards her, then lifted the lid. "It looks divine. Can I hold it?"

Without waiting for an answer, Joan picked the gun up right from the case and inspected it. "Well, if you're going to go armed, you might as well make it gorgeous. How do I get my hands on a pretty little thing like this? Have you fired it yet?"

"No, I haven't. And I was just about to put it away," Penelope said, taking the gun from Joan and placing it back into the case again. She firmly closed both the lid and the side compartment with the bullets. "There's a bookshelf in Agnes's room I can hide it behind during the party. Are you happy now, Richard?"

"You may want to keep it on you, Penelope, after all,

there is a murderer in Long Island," Joan said, giving everyone a spooky look.

"Is there?" Richard asked, his brow arched questioningly.

Penelope told everyone about Martha's having been run over and how the police thought it was murder.

"So she was a maid working for a home over in Sands Point, yet she was killed just up the road from here?" Richard asked. Penelope knew he was confirming facts that once again made James look rather suspect.

"Yes, but the police already questioned us, and the only car here at the time was driven by Leonard, which they made sure to thoroughly inspect. Unless of course, you suspect my chauffeur of foul play, detective?" She asked pointedly.

"Not at all," he replied, just as pointedly.

"Detective, you say? How convenient," Joan said, eyeing him with delight in her eyes. Richard didn't seem quite as amused.

"So are you going to introduce us to yet even more new friends?" Benny asked now that there was something more interesting for him to focus on. He cast his eyes towards James who had walked Savannah further away. "Though it looks like those two are already well acquainted."

"This is Joan Dyson, Bruce Carlton's cousin," Pen said, gesturing to the woman who was walking to the bar to help herself to the gin leftover from the French 75 cocktails.

"Not to worry, Brucie and I are nothing alike."

"Which instantly earns you a mark of approval in my book," Benny said as she brought over the entire bottle and took the seat James had vacated. Having grown up in the same circles as Pen, Benny would know the Carlton family and Bruce in particular. Benny had probably been an easy target for Bruce's torment when they were children. "Benny Davenport."

"Pleasure to meet you, Benny-Boy," Joan said, taking his hand. She introduced herself to everyone else. In the ensuing silence, everyone turned to where James and Savannah were standing off to the side in a rather intimate tableau.

"That would be Savannah Duncan, Bruce's intended wife," Joan said with a smirk.

"I would say her *intentions* lie elsewhere," Lulu mused.

"It serves Bruce right," Joan said in a blithe tone. "It isn't as if he hasn't been happily plowing the fields of Long Island all summer."

Savannah sighed, having overheard that, and took one step away from James. "Really, Joan."

"It doesn't matter," James said pulling her back to his side. "You're here now."

Savannah brought her gaze back to him and her eyes softened with adoration. "Yes, I am."

"Perhaps you two would like a room?" Joan suggested with a laugh. "I think there might be one or two available in this *grandiose* mansion."

"We could perhaps go for a walk," James suggested, staring intently at Savannah.

Her eyelashes fluttered and a timid smile came to her face. "I think I'd like that."

"You'll excuse us?" James turned to say to the group before taking her hand and walking her away.

"Was coming here tonight your idea or hers?" Penelope asked Joan, a note of cynicism in her voice.

"A little of this, a little of that," Joan replied with a wave of the hand. "If you're worried about aiding and abetting any indiscretion, no need to worry. If anything, this is likely to make Bruce even more eager to walk down the aisle. He's completely insufferable when it comes to competition—win at all costs. In which case, brava Savannah. The gal certainly knows how to play her cards right."

"Why *are* they getting married?"

Joan grinned over her glass. "You mean you didn't notice how desperately devoted the betrothed were this morning?"

"I must have missed that," Penelope said wryly.

Joan laughed and sipped her gin before responding. "Brucie-boy gets complete access to his trust fund if he marries, now that his twenty-fifth birthday has come and gone. Otherwise, he'd have to wait until he's thirty. Unless of course, he misbehaves in a manner of which dear grand-*mama* disapproves. He is a favorite of hers, for some ungodly reason, so the bar is quite high. The old biddy positively adores ill-mannered boys. Not quite so forgiving when it comes to us gals. I've already been cut off multiple times over.

"As for why Bruce picked Savannah? Well, he and Finn went to Yale together. They became friendly enough that he'd met her once or twice and liked what he saw. I suspect it's the demure southern belle appeal. Though, I have my suspicions he might be rudely surprised once those vows are taken. There's a bit of mettle in that one."

"But why is Savannah marrying *Bruce*?" Benny asked, voicing the incredulity Penelope was feeling.

"Again, money. A tale as old as time. I don't know all the details but from the way Finn frets about, I suspect the Duncan family is a fading violet, at least as far as finances go."

That was as much as Penelope suspected.

"Any other family secrets you'd like me to divulge?"

THE GREAT GASTON MURDER

Joan teased, leaning back and crossing one leg over the other. "I'd much rather focus on this upcoming party of yours. Will it be as fabulous as the prior owner's were?"

"Have you ever attended one of Agnes's parties?"

"Oh yes. A shame about her accident. Luckily the new wing she had added to the house doesn't ruin the aesthetic at all." Pen frowned with disapproval. Joan simply continued as though she hadn't said anything insensitive. "Still, I have to give credit to the old gal, she knew how to throw a real humdinger, even after that. Quite the shoes to fill, my dear."

"Well, no one could replace Agnes. Still, I'm happy to honor her memory by doing my best. I hadn't realized just how much goes into planning these things."

"That's what the roaring twenties is about, darling. One wonders how long this party will go on. Fitzgerald published a rather interesting take on such hedonism in his latest."

"*The Great Gatsby*? You've read it?" Penelope asked in surprise. The book had only been published a few months ago. As far as Pen could tell, it hadn't been very popular, even though it had received mostly favorable reviews.

"Don't let the gorgeous facade fool you, there is a brain in this head," Joan said tapping her temple. "And yes it does like to read books. I found it rather delicious. You do realize he was mocking the overindulgence and shallowness of wealthy society? I suspect it was a critique, not an ode."

"You don't say!" Penelope responded with mock astonishment.

Joan offered an apologetic laugh. "I suppose I shouldn't patronize my hostess. No offense meant."

"None taken. Though Fitzgerald will be happy to learn

that this time next year, this estate will be dedicated to injured veterans. So feel free to revel without guilt."

"Why do I suddenly feel under attack?" Benny said with pursed lips. "I, for one, love being part of the idle rich. Struggle is far too overrated. One of the very reasons I have yet to read any of F. Scott's work. Only he could make wealth seem like a tragedy. I swear, the man is enamored of his own wretchedness. Please don't tell me you've caught that ailment, Pen, you're far too interesting for that. I blame that wife of his, Zelda—I met her at a party once. He's a fool in love, and *she's* positively mad."

"Speaking of fools in love," Joan said, before finishing off the rest of her drink. "At some point, I suppose I should go and rescue our fair maiden from the clutches of the usurper."

"Before Bruce misses her," Pen said pointedly.

"He's taken Finn and Morris and jetted off somewhere, no doubt to Manhattan for a bit of fun." She arched an eyebrow as though that needed no interpretation. "That's why we had to come by boat."

Suddenly this engagement of theirs seemed even more entangled. All Pen had expected was a quiet but fun weekend and then a fabulous party. First, there had been this tragic business with Martha Combs being murdered. Now she was spun up in a web that even a spider couldn't weave. She just hoped this tale didn't end as tragically as Fitzgerald's new book had.

An hour or so later, everyone had either retired to their rooms or boated back to their part of Long Island. Everything had been removed from the terrace, including the candles, which left only the few lights on in the house to see by.

Penelope and Richard stole a moment for themselves at the end of the dock, enjoying the peace and quiet and each other.

"Are you still upset about the gun?"

"No, your friend Lulu is right, you should have one. I'm more upset about its origins. Who knows what criminal activity it may have been involved in?"

Pen laughed. "I hardly see any of Jack Sweeney's cronies sporting a small, jade gun, do you?"

A slow, reluctant grin came to his face. "I suppose not. But I'm taking you to a shooting range myself to at least get you trained on that thing. No need to have an unfortunate accident with it."

"There now, see how easily we resolve issues?" Pen tilted her head up at him with a smile.

"There's also this James Gaston. The *artist*," Richard said in a dry voice not looking too pleased. "How well do you know him?"

"Don't tell me you're jealous," she teased.

"No, just...cautious."

"I'm not a complete fool, you know. I did check up on him." Pen repeated not only everything James had told her himself, but what she'd learned from Chives and Mr. Wilcox. "Can we go back to celebrating my birthday?"

"Yes, we can. In fact, I can think of a perfect way to celebrate, something slightly more enjoyable than this," he said with a daring grin.

"And here I thought I said no presents. That would make two in one night."

He frowned. "Heaven help me if it's only two."

Penelope coughed out a scandalized laugh. "Why Detective Prescott, now who's the naughty one?"

"On that note, I'm afraid I'll have to put my detective hat back on and accompany you back to your room ma'am. I need to make sure that gun is safely stored away. Just for good measure, I'll probably need to search you for other contraband."

"I suppose I have no choice, detective. The law is the law," Penelope said in an overly flirtatious voice.

They both laughed and he took her hand, leading her back toward the house. As they headed down the dock, Penelope looked out on the water to the west. She could just make out the cottage where James was staying. There was a tiny orange flicker of a match being lit, and she realized James was standing on the small front porch to smoke a cigarette. He was turned west towards Sands Point. She followed his gaze which was presumably trained on the Carlton home out of all the others along the coast. There was one light glowing from a room on the second floor. Like most of the other windows, that one had a stained glass transom window that now glowed green in the night. Pen didn't have to guess whose room that was.

CHAPTER TEN

THE NEXT MORNING, PENELOPE HAD RECOVERED WELL enough from the night's activities—Richard had done the gentlemanly thing and wrangled up a cup of coffee to bring to her in bed before quietly escaping back to his bedroom—to meet with the organizer who was responsible for putting the party together, Gilda Windfall. The weather was still quite overcast, and last night there had been a good hard rainstorm, which didn't bode well for the next day's celebrations. Still, Penelope was optimistic.

"Miss Banks!" Gilda sang with a wide smile as Chives led her into the parlor where Penelope had been waiting for her. She was flamboyantly dressed in a short silk kimono with a loud floral pattern and black harem pants. She had a silver turban on her head and matching silver bangles going up each arm that clanked and jingled against each other. Her nails were lacquered in dark green and her eyes were slathered in kohl. It presented a rather startling picture and she certainly had the personality to go with it.

"I was *so devastated* when I heard of Agnes's demise," she crooned as she greeted Penelope. Gilda grasped her offered hand in both of hers and squeezed. "The moment suicide was mentioned I *knew* something sinister was afoot. Agnes would have never left us in such a platitudinous manner. Bless you for uncovering the *dastardly* truth!"

"Yes, well..." Penelope said hesitantly, "all the more reason to do her memory justice with this party. As you know, this will most likely be the last one held here."

"The travesty of it!" Gilda lamented, the back of her hand coming up to her forehead. The bangles tinkled in an incongruously cheerful manner. Penelope had the frightening idea that she might actually faint. She recovered quickly, her attention homing in on Penelope once again. "Rest assured, Miss Banks, this party will be the talk of Long Island for at least a decade!"

"Hopefully in a good way," Penelope said with a forced smile. "And please call me Penelope."

Gilda trilled with laughter, then clapped her hands together with sudden seriousness. "As I stated when you first contacted me, you're going to leave everything to Gilda. You, my dear, won't have to lift a pretty little finger, simply show up and be your *marvelous* self," she sang waving her hand in the air yet again. "But allow me to walk you through the details. It's going to be quite the *busy buzzing* day of preparation! A party like this requires a fair amount of bells and whistles, nuts and bolts, and such and such! But the result will be a *masterpiece*." She threw her hands out so spectacularly Pen flinched, worried the bangles would fly off in every direction.

An hour later Penelope found herself exhausted. Just being near Gilda was akin to running a marathon. She was still a bundle of indefatigable excitement as she continued.

"Now then, the eastern dancers will be in each corner of the foyer. The acrobats will hang from the ceiling. Don't worry about the chandelier, darling, it won't be touched! The fire eaters will of course be outside on the terrace along with the jugglers. And there will be sparklers everywhere! It will be a carnival of delights!"

The mention of a carnival sparked something in Pen's mind. "How many years did you work with Agnes?"

A deep frown came to Gilda's face and her eyes narrowed as she studied Penelope. "I may be a certain age, young lady, but that doesn't mean I'm not aware of modern trends, particularly with regard to parties."

"Oh no, I wasn't implying anything about your age or abilities. I just had a question about one of Agnes's past parties; one that may have taken place perhaps twenty-five years ago or so?"

"Just how *old* do you think I am?" Gilda exclaimed, her hand to her chest with umbrage.

"I was thinking perhaps you knew the individual who worked with her during that time," Penelope hedged, doing her best to repair the damage to Gilda's pride. "I was curious as to whether they might have hired directly from any carnivals that would have been passing through at the time."

Gilda gasped as though Pen had committed blasphemy. "*Gypsy criminals?* Agnes might as well have invited Bolshevik *communists* to work at the party. *They* at least have the decency to *tell* you they're stealing from you. No, no my dear, rest assured, anyone employed by Gilda Windfall has been thoroughly vetted and verified."

"Oh, I'm not worried about theft or anything of that sort. I trust you completely. But, just to be clear, the parties that took place around the turn of the century had similar standards?"

"That was most definitely before my time, mind you,"

she said, squinting one eye at Pen as though daring her to contradict. "But I do know the person who worked with Agnes then. He was the one who transferred her into the safe hands of yours truly once he retired. I can *firmly* state that Walter would have never, *ever* hired anyone from a *passing carnival*." She uttered the words as though talking about horse droppings.

"I see, well, I feel reassured already," Penelope said, plastering a smile on her face.

Still, she was perfectly perplexed. James had said his mother worked at one of Agnes's parties, and that was how they had met. Yes, it had seemed somewhat implausible at the time, if only for the coincidence of it all. Agnes had been rather eccentric and generous to all, no matter what their station. Thus, Pen hadn't immediately dismissed the idea. Now, it seemed that it had been a lie. So what *was* Agnes's relationship to James's mother, or rather, James himself?

The sound of the doorbell filled the foyer, and Chives answered it. Pen hadn't been expecting anyone else today and any of the delivery workers would have used a side entrance. Standing on the landing beyond the open door was an older gentleman, perhaps in his sixties. He was handsome, with hair that had gone completely white under his hat, a nicely trimmed beard, and an ingratiating smile on his face. He wore a fine suit, fit for summer. His wasn't a face familiar to Penelope and she turned to Gilda with an inquiring look.

"My, my," Gilda muttered, staring at the man with undisguised fascination, which meant she didn't know him either.

"Good day," he said to Chives, removing his hat and offering a slight bow. "I'm sorry to arrive unannounced, but

THE GREAT GASTON MURDER

I'm here to inquire about a guest I believe is staying on the property. A Mr. James Gaston?"

At the mention of that name, Penelope walked over to introduce herself.

"Hello, I'm Penelope Banks."

From a closer distance, he was even more handsome, with a cheerful expression. What struck her were his bright green eyes that had an almost hypnotic lure. They twinkled as they settled on her.

"Miss Banks, it's a pleasure to meet you. The name's Lawrence Whittaker."

"How do you know James?"

"I happen to represent Mr. Gaston in his artistic endeavors, at least on this side of the pond," he said with a laugh.

His good humor was contagious and Penelope smiled. "Well, it's very nice to meet you, Mr. Whittaker. James is staying in one of the cottages here. Why don't you come in while I send for him?"

"I certainly didn't mean to intrude on your day," he said giving her an apologetic look. His eyes flitted to Gilda who made a sudden appearance next to her. "Although I can't say I'm disappointed at having my day brightened with such lovely creatures as those I am presently blessed by."

If this was how he operated in selling James's work, it was no wonder he was such a success, even beyond his talent. This man could charm even the most cynical buyer.

"Nonsense," Penelope said urging him in. "We were just going over the plans for the party taking place tomorrow."

"A party that *I* am organizing," Gilda added with flair. She reached out a hand. "Gilda Windfall—*Miss* Gilda Windfall, should you ever need my *services*."

Pen had to keep from rolling her eyes at the suggestion. But Lawrence was more than happy to play along. He took hold of her hand and kissed the back of it like a perfect gentleman. "I do not doubt your many talents, *mademoiselle*."

Gilda tittered in response. Pen asked Chives to have someone send for James while Gilda detailed the more interesting highlights of the upcoming party.

"I must say this party of yours sounds like quite the experience," Mr. Whittaker said.

"It's for my twenty-fifth birthday."

"My, my! Well, my dear, a very happy birthday to you," he said twirling his hat and bowing again.

"As you're a friend of James, and he's coming, why don't you come as well? The invitation is already open to almost everyone."

"Yes, yes you *must* come!" Gilda said clasping her hands together with joy. "It's to be *the* event to end the summer with a bang!"

"In that case, how can I refuse?" he said, his eyes aglitter.

Gilda continued to regale him with descriptions of the party. Penelope was just happy for the momentary respite.

"What the hell are you doing here?"

They all turned at the sound of James's voice to find him entering through the back French doors. Penelope's brow wrinkled in confusion at the expression of contempt on his face as he stared at Lawrence.

"James, my dear boy. I came by to visit after learning you had returned to the states. I wish you would have let me know you were coming back," Lawrence said not looking at all put out by James's less than warm reception.

"Yes, well..." James said, his face quickly smoothing over

as he remembered they weren't alone. "It was a last-minute decision."

"Apparently," Lawrence said with a chuckle. "But how fortuitous to find you here at dear Agnes's home."

James's smile disappeared as he came closer. "How did you find out I was back?"

"Oh James, you know how gossip runs in our world. There are no secrets," Lawrence responded with a wink and a good-humored chuckle.

"I took the liberty of inviting Mr. Whittaker to the party Saturday, I hope you don't mind?" Penelope asked with uncertainty.

James looked more resigned than anything, which was odd. He forced a smile. "Of course I don't mind. After all, I wouldn't be where I am today without Lawrence," he said tightly.

"Well, then..." Penelope said unsure of what else to add.

"Why don't you come back to the cottage?" James said to him in a terse voice. "You can view my latest work and we can discuss promoting it here in America."

"A fine idea!" Lawrence said still as amicable as ever. He bowed once towards Gilda who giggled like a schoolgirl. "*Miss* Gilda Windfall, it has been a delight."

Then, he turned to Penelope, taking her hand and kissing the back of it. "It was a pleasure to meet you, Miss Banks. I look forward to helping you celebrate the culmination of your twenty-fifth year of life this coming Saturday."

Penelope thanked him, and James quickly led him back outside.

"My, what a devastatingly charming man," Gilda said, hand pressed to her chest as she watched them walk off.

"He certainly is," Penelope agreed in a distracted way.

She replayed the interaction between Lawrence and

James in her head. James certainly hadn't been happy about Lawrence's appearance. And Lawrence seemed to delight in having caught James off guard with his surprise appearance. She knew that there were often spats or disagreements between agents and the artists they represented, often by nature of the temperament of many artists. However, James was rather sanguine about life, and Lawrence seemed incapable of being rattled. What was the true nature of their relationship? Did it have anything to do with Agnes? Pen just hoped they settled whatever differences they had before tomorrow's party.

Then again, perhaps she could put on her private detective hat to find out more.

CHAPTER ELEVEN

PENELOPE WAITED A GOOD TWENTY MINUTES BEFORE making her way to James's cottage. She had hoped whatever disagreement he had with Lawrence would have been smoothed over by then. She didn't want any discord at her party, at least not any more than there would already be, what with the troublesome love triangle of James, Savannah, and Bruce.

When the cottage came into view, she was surprised to hear James and Lawrence still arguing. She thought about backtracking and waiting for a more appropriate moment, until she caught some of the exchange.

"I won't do it, I already told you. Did you think coming here unannounced would change my mind?" James yelled.

"I thought coming here would remind you of your obligations." Lawrence didn't sound quite so charming now. His low, threatening tone sent a shiver through Penelope.

"I don't owe you a damn thing."

"Oh, I think you do." The way Lawrence chuckled this time had a sinister edge to it.

"We were done a long time ago. Nothing has changed."

"Everything has changed. Now, you're here with *her*? Suddenly, you want to throw it all away? I don't think so, my boy."

So he was upset about Savannah then. Perhaps Lawrence thought she might have a bad influence on James's art. Or, more likely, she was a distraction from him completing it.

"I'm not throwing it all away. I'm simply going in a new direction, one that suits me. It is *my* life after all. I love Savannah and she loves me. I'm going to do right by her, and I'm not letting anything get in the way of that, not even you."

There was a long pause, and Penelope could almost sense the heat of resentment radiating from the cottage.

"I could make trouble, you know, make things very difficult for you."

James breathed out a laugh. "You do and that will be the end of everything. We'll be done, *over*. I'm not without my own ammunition, after all."

"Is that a threat?"

"Consider it in whatever way has you leaving this alone." There was another pause before James spoke again in a lower voice. "I'm doing things my way. And when I do, you and I are done. Don't bother with threats, they don't mean anything to me, not anymore. Savannah knows everything there is to know about me...and you."

"I see all those years in that foreign country have emboldened you. Well, I certainly hope you're able to back up that bark with a bite, my boy."

"Just go. You've said what you came to say. I'm not changing my mind."

"We'll just see about that."

Penelope noted the hint of finality in that statement and quickly backtracked to the main house to avoid detection, assuming Mr. Whittaker intended to leave on the heels of that.

What had that been about? Owing dues? And what had Mr. Whittaker meant by making trouble for James?

It was nearly lunchtime and James was set to join her friends and her. However, the hour arrived and he didn't make an appearance. Penelope and the others waited until it was obvious he wasn't going to come, then continued without him.

Afterward, Penelope had a plate made for him and insisted on taking it to his cottage herself. She didn't hear any voices this time, so she approached the door and knocked.

"James? I've brought a plate of lunch for you," she announced.

After a moment, he opened the door, greeting her with a welcome smile, as though nothing upsetting had happened at all.

"Sorry I didn't make it. Lawrence and I were still discussing...which paintings of mine should be selected for a show."

"Were you?" Pen asked, handing the plate to him.

"Thank you," he said as he accepted it. Pen followed him into the small kitchenette area of the cottage. He placed the plate down on the table but didn't take a seat. Instead, he paced, rubbing the back of his neck. His face was contorted in thought. "I'm sorry about him showing up unannounced like that."

"Don't be. You don't mind that I invited him to the party do you?"

He exhaled. "Well, it's done now. It would be more of a

problem if you revoked it at this point." He stopped pacing to face her. "Just...try not to become too enamored of him, Penelope. He has a way of luring you in and then taking advantage."

"Has he done that with you?"

"Only once he saw I had some value," he said bitterly.

"Who is he to you?"

James stared at her for a long moment as though wondering if he should answer that.

"It's just that, I *may* have overheard some of your argument. About you owing him?"

His brow rose in surprise, then he smiled as though he approved of her eavesdropping. It quickly disappeared before he spoke.

"Lawrence is...someone from my days at the carnival. He was the reason my mother tried to get me out. He's not a good man."

This told Penelope nothing at all, and yet...

She thought back to the man she'd met. He was older, but there was a certain spryness about him. He was a practiced charmer, enough so that perhaps twenty-three or so years ago, he might have poured enough of it on to lure a young woman into something untoward. After all, Pen's father was fifteen years older than her mother had been when they were married. Depending on how old James's mother had been, it was probably a more significant age difference, but nothing unheard of.

"Is he your father?"

James met her with a wry smile, as though expecting that question. "My mother claims she doesn't know who my father is. But one thing I am certain of is that Lawrence *isn't* my father. There are very few secrets in the carnie world, and that's definitely something I would have heard whispered about early on. No, Lawrence is nothing more than a relic from my past. One I plan on finally ridding myself of, once and for all."

There was a set look to his face that hinted at something dark and dangerous—if it came to that.

"If it's just money you need, James, I can help you. Heaven knows Agnes left me enough. Perhaps I'll just pay far too much for one of your paintings. If Agnes liked your work, you must at least have talent."

"*No*, not for him, Penelope." He shook his head vehemently, then stopped to pierce her with his gaze. "Don't ever connect yourself to him that way, not even through me. Once he has his hooks in you it's impossible to release yourself."

"He wouldn't be the first person who tried to use me for money," she said with a laugh.

James didn't laugh in return. "I've spent my whole life around people like him, Penelope. Have you ever been to a carnival?"

"I've been to Coney Island," she offered with a bit of humor.

"I mean a proper traveling show. The kind that drops in to milk a town, then just as quickly picks up camp and moves on to the next city of marks? The kind with tents making wild promises for a show, and booths offering big prizes for hitting the right target?"

"What about it?"

"There's always a con going on, Penelope. That's what you have to be wary of. You toss the ring, never realizing that the head of the bottle for the grand prize is too big for it to fit. You pay your nickel, only to find that the bearded lady is a man in a dress."

He became even more somber. "You don't even realize

it when the fortune teller gets you talking, finds out your fears and dreams then tells you exactly what you want to hear." James laughed softly, bitterly. "Or just enough to get you to buy a love potion, a good luck charm, or some quack medicine for what ails you. Lawrence is the king of the con, Penelope. It's all a performance. Don't be fooled by his charm. He'll try to use it on you tomorrow if he can. Don't fall for it."

"I guess I've been properly warned," she said. Pen tilted her head to consider him. "As for you, how do you intend on paying what's due? Do you have any money?"

"I will soon enough," he muttered, a look of resolve in his eyes.

"Through your art?" Pen asked, pleased about that.

A bitter smile came to his face. "Yes indeed, Pen."

Penelope had the feeling there was a hidden meaning in his response. It certainly didn't do anything to alleviate her concerns.

"He seemed upset about Savannah," she said, moving on.

James wrinkled his brow, looking bewildered.

"I may have overheard that part too," she clarified with a guilty smile. "About you throwing it all away for her."

A crooked smile of understanding came to his face. "As you might imagine, he doesn't approve. Thinks my efforts are better spent elsewhere."

That was understandable. Still, she didn't like the threatening tone Lawrence had used or that warning about having the ammunition to ruin James. Pen briefly flirted with the idea of asking him about that but figured she had pried enough for one day.

"You and Savannah, are you sure you know what you're doing?"

James's gaze sharpened, piercing her with a fierceness that she found unsettling. "I'm doing what's best for both of us, Penelope. Trust me."

CHAPTER TWELVE

"Happy Birthday!"

"Hey, great party, Pen!"

"Are you the one throwing this party? It's the absolute berries!"

"Happy birthday!"

"Thank you!" Penelope replied for perhaps the hundredth time tonight, this time to someone she didn't even know. It really was like a Gatsby party; very few had been directly invited, they had just arrived.

Penelope should have been pleased. Even the weather was cooperating, the sun finally making an appearance after nothing but clouds overhead for the past two days and nights. Up above, the moon was finally providing its own bit of festive, glowing light.

As for the party, it was a success, at least going by attendance. She knew it was more curiosity than anything resembling personal affection for the hostess that had people coming out. Penelope was a rare breed indeed, someone who had been cut off by her father, somehow made a living for several years in a way that whispered rumors claimed was illegal, and was then gifted enough money to make many of the Vanderbilts (some of whom were in attendance) green with envy. Of course everyone would take advantage of the open invitation.

Looking around, Penelope thought Agnes would approve of the spectacle. Outside, buffet tables had been piled with a variety of food from hors-d'oeuvres to elegant tarts and all the courses in between. Twenty different kinds of colorful salads, platters of finger sandwiches, piles of fruit artfully arranged, and every kind of meat to satisfy one's preference. There was even a large roasted pig. Along with the tarts, the dessert tables consisted of dainty petit fours, cakes with so many layers they threatened to topple over, and jars filled with colorful candy as far as the eye could see. There was even an ice cream bar.

Inside, the parlor served as the main alcohol station with at least twenty tenders taking orders. Islands of smaller bars were dotted throughout the property, each making a different signature drink conjured up by an expert Gilda had hired just for the occasion. Pen had made sure one of them served French 75s the way James had made them.

The entertainment was indeed a delight for the eyes, and all the other senses as well. Performers could be found every which way someone turned. Inside, scantily clad acrobats hung from swings bolted to the ceilings, burlesque performers with feathered fans and eastern dancers with colorful scarves mesmerized the eyes. Fire-eaters and jugglers elicited *oohs* and *ahhs*. Flappers and the boys who adored them created their own impromptu shows on the dance floor. Balloons, streamers, and confetti covered every surface. A jazz band, large enough to make the one at the

Peacock Club seem barebones, filled the air with lively music.

The crowd itself was an exhibition: authors, politicians, actors, millionaires, athletes, socialites, and gangsters all partied on equal footing with the people who usually serviced them. It was a hodgepodge, mishmash, melange of attendees that covered every letter in the alphabet from the Astors to Ziegfeld girls.

And Penelope herself sparkled, wearing a gold and black beaded dress with an intricate design and edged in fringe that swished with festive flair when she so much as took a step.

"Why Pen Banks, the party is everything I expected and more, brava!" Joan slinked her way around to greet her. She was unsurprisingly wearing a men's tuxedo, complete with a top hat and her trademark cigarette holder. She'd thrown in a monocle just for a bit of fun.

"So, you came," Pen said with a grin.

"Wouldn't miss it, darling. We all came, in fact. Even Finn has managed to loosen that stiff shirt of his, though I suspect he's only here to spy on his sister's actions. I believe Brucie and Morrie are presently drowning themselves in a pool of blondes." She gave Pen a sly look. "Then again, I don't think our Savie would mind very much, do you? She seems to be drowning all on her own. If she isn't careful she may not come up for air."

"I try not to meddle in the affairs of others," Pen said pointedly. She certainly didn't want her night ruined by that mess, which she was beginning to rue having played even a minor role in.

"Touché," Joan said, lifting her glass. "At any rate, Pen darling, fabulous shindig! I'm going to continue exploring. Someone said they saw Louise Brooks riding a zebra?"

"It wouldn't surprise me," Pen said with a laugh, though it was more likely one of any number of flappers who mimicked the style of the famous star.

Pen accepted Joan's parting air kiss and continued on her way through the crowd, accepting birthday wishes from those who managed to recognize her. She saw Alfred Paisley from afar, his head rising above the crowd.

She rushed over to greet him. "Alfie, you came!"

"Yes, thankfully there was a conveyer belt of hired cars transporting people from the train station. It was all very convenient," he said, pushing his glasses up on his nose. His gorgeous green eyes searched the crowd looking for one face in particular. Jane's romance with Alfred Paisley, from their last murder case, had moved surprisingly fast, in a quaint sort of way. Hopefully, it would lead to something lasting. After all, Paisley was far superior to Pugley as a last name. Besides, much like Penelope, Jane had been rather unlucky in love and deserved someone wonderful. Alfred was smart, considerate, sensible, and seemed to adore her.

"Not to worry, Jane is safely keeping Cousin Cordelia company," she hinted. They both knew how low Jane's tolerance for alcohol was. "Other than the one glass of champagne, she won't be tempted by anything other than the occasional nip of brandy. I think I saw them outside marveling at the fire eaters."

"Yes," he said, swallowing hard as he always did when the subject of Jane came up. "Oh, er, happy birthday, Penelope."

"Pen, please, at this point we're friends. And congratulations on finally taking the bar, I suppose?"

"Congratulate me when I get the results."

"I doubt you of all people need it."

Alfred, never one to be afflicted with false modesty,

THE GREAT GASTON MURDER

smiled and nodded in thanks, then escaped to find the only woman here who could leave him jingle-brained. Pen watched him leave with a satisfied smile. That was at least one love affair that held promise.

She continued to mingle, catching glimpses here and there of people she knew, or knew through others, or knew simply because they were famous—or infamous.

She saw Lulu looking fabulous as always in a glittery gold number, dancing it up with a member of the band who was on break.

She saw Benny instructing one of the young bartenders on how to make a particular drink for him. She suspected there was more going on than simple instruction, perhaps some esoteric mating ritual of those "so inclined" that the rest of society wouldn't know about.

She saw Cousin Cordelia nipping away at a glass of brandy and, contrary to her usual blue-nosed disapproval, gleefully enjoying one of the scantily clad acrobats who contorted herself above her in the foyer.

Near her, she saw Alfie finally catching up with Jane—tonight in a sparkling blue dress that transformed her from a wallflower into an orchid—then stealing a kiss.

Though she wasn't looking, she did find Bruce with Morris and Finn, indeed in a group of giggling blonde flappers. One would have never known he had just announced his engagement, from the looks of things. Still, the grouping was enough to attract even more zozzled boys to the cluster.

"Save some for the rest of us, Bruce! You've already got a pretty little blonde waiting for you," one of them said in a boisterous, yet slurred voice.

"Never such a thing as too many blondes!" Bruce replied lifting his glass with a laugh.

"And you Morris, aren't you supposed to be in Nantucket?"

"Newport, you mug. And I bloused that town. No parties like this out there!"

"Newport, Nantucket, either way, New York still has the best blondes!"

"Here here!"

The men laughed. The women giggled. Everyone drank. Zounds, they were sloshed Pen thought as she quickly moved on.

"I'm kidnapping you," Pen heard someone whisper in her ear, just before a strong pair of arms encircled her waist.

She laughed and leaned back into Richard, feeling herself finally relax. They had lost each other during her duties as hostess. Now, she was all his again. Pen laughed again when he walked further inside, his tall, strong presence doing a better job of cutting through the thick crowd than she ever could. She noted he was walking her toward the small hallway that led to Agnes's bedroom, the one place on the first floor where they could snatch a moment of privacy. This hallway and those upstairs leading to the other bedrooms were guarded by men who kept the partiers from going where they weren't supposed to.

Tonight was the first time Penelope had seen Richard in a tuxedo and he looked even more handsome, something she didn't think possible. She couldn't wait to get another full look of him in it again. Maybe get it a tad wrinkled during a few stolen moments of whoopee.

Before they could get there, a ruckus erupted in the crowd near the front door. The sound of a man shouting reached her ears, even above the laughter, chatter, and music. Behind her, Pen felt Richard go tense, no doubt putting his detective hat back on to handle the man who sounded like he was itching for a fight.

"Where is he? I know he's here somewhere! I'm going to kill him!"

CHAPTER THIRTEEN

Richard released Penelope and once again cut through the crowd, this time toward the open front doors. She followed him. He came to a stop in front of a man who was already quite drunk. He was perhaps in his late twenties, with black hair, strands of which fell into his eyes. With his soft chin, round cheeks, and snub nose, he had a baby face that was now red with rage.

"Calm down," Richard said with authority, taking the man by the shoulder and leading him away.

"No, I won't! I know that bastard is here," he said, shaking off his hand.

"Who are you talking about?"

"James Gaston!" He craned his neck to see if he could spot him.

Pen's interest was now even more piqued. What did this man want with James? For someone who was a stranger to Long Island, and frankly New York, he was awfully popular.

"What's your name?" Richard asked, mostly to get him to settle down.

"Darren Combs."

Martha Combs's husband then. He had apparently received the news about his wife's murder. But why did he blame James?

In the wake of this tirade, the noise of the crowd had quieted enough to hear the conversation. Outside, partiers were still oblivious, the laughter and music continuing. But one person had heard his name or at least had been made aware.

"What is it you want with me?" Penelope heard James's voice call out. He appeared in the crowd, closely followed by Savannah. When he made his way to the small clearing, he stared at Darren showing no recognition. "Who are you?"

"Are you James Gaston?"

"I am. Again, who are you?"

Rather than answer, Darren pushed Richard out of the way and lunged at James with a roar.

"You killed her! You murdered my wife, my beautiful Martha!"

As though expecting it, James sidestepped him and easily evaded the attack. He was taller and not nearly as drunk, so when Darren came for him again, he once again avoided any major impact.

Richard took hold of Darren once again, this time, securing him with both arms in a bear hug. He was a force to contain, still raging and kicking out at James, who stood there completely dumbfounded at the accusation.

"Calm down, Mr. Combs."

The energy of the crowd was rising again at this little show, people hungrily curious about this announcement of murder. The vulgar idea that there might be something scandalous attached to it only fueled them.

Penelope gave Richard a look and he nodded in response, as though reading her thoughts. She walked over to James and rested a hand on his shoulder.

"Let's go back outside."

Behind her, she could hear Richard handling Darren. "Alright, Mr. Combs, let's go get some fresh air, and talk this out, shall we?"

While he and Darren went back out the front doors, Penelope led James out back through the open French doors. Everyone turned to stare, now even those who hadn't witnessed the brief altercation. The whispers began to spread.

"How about a more private location?" she suggested, leading him down the steps and west toward his cottage. Savannah wordlessly followed them. When they reached the cottage, they stood on the small little porch that faced the water.

"Why would he think I killed his wife? I didn't even know her," James said, looking perplexed. His attention was understandably on Savannah, as though reassuring her that he wasn't involved with this woman.

"Someone put a little whisper in his ear." Pen eyed Savannah, as though hinting as to whom that might have been.

"It wouldn't surprise me if Bruce did something that underhanded. He's been spending so much time with Morris, and I'm sure by now the Belmont family has been made aware of the murder."

"According to Morris, he loved her dearly. That's bound to make someone outraged, especially if they've been drinking, and Darren most certainly has been."

"Your, er, detective friend, surely he doesn't suspect I did it, does he?"

"No, of course not. Richard has more common sense than that. Anyone looking at the facts could tell it wasn't you. You didn't even have a car, and there's no evidence you even knew her. You've been in Paris until only this past week, correct?"

"Yes," he insisted.

"Still, what was she doing here, on this side of the island," Savannah asked.

James rushed over to her. "Savannah, I didn't kill her."

"I know, love," she assured him, reaching a hand up to cup his face. "I just have to wonder how far someone might go to frame you. Perhaps if they knew about us?"

"You think Bruce drove her out this way just to kill her and frame James?" Pen asked. "That seems like an awful lot of trouble to go through. And why do it on Brookline Drive instead of closer to the estate, just to make sure the blame landed here? Do you even have reason to suspect Bruce knew about you two at that point?"

Pen recalled the sudden awareness in Bruce's eyes when he put James together with the painting of Savannah in their sitting room. Before that, he didn't show any hint of recognition.

"Oh, I don't know," Savanah sighed, falling onto the chair on the porch.

James fell to his knees before her and took her hands. "Whatever it is, it has nothing to do with us. It changes nothing."

She finally dragged her eyes up to stare into his and some bit of understanding passed between them. She eventually smiled and nodded. "Of course, love."

Somewhere nearby the sound of someone clearing their throat sounded. They all turned to find Joan approaching, an amused look on her face. "I hate to break

THE GREAT GASTON MURDER

up this little tryst, but I've been tasked with collecting the birthday girl. It seems the main event of the night is set to take place?"

"Ah yes, the fireworks," Pen said, though the last thing she felt right now was festive. Being reminded of Martha's murder had cast a dour cloud over her thoughts. It was a tragedy, made all the more so, since there didn't seem to be any suspects.

"I'll leave you two here," she said, descending from the porch to join Joan.

"Nonsense," James said, standing back up. Savannah joined him. "We certainly aren't going to ruin your party with this nonsense."

"Are you sure?"

"Yes," Savannah said, taking James's hand. "Besides, I love fireworks."

They all headed back toward the terrace of the main house where the crowd had gathered in anticipation of the show. Bruce saw the four of them and stormed over. He practically snatched Savannah away from James. "What the hell is this?"

"You'd be wise to keep your hands off her," James said, stepping in closer to him.

"No, James, let me handle this," Savannah said, settling him with nothing more than a light hand on his arm. She turned to Bruce. "Let's talk somewhere private."

James didn't look pleased. Joan certainly did, biting back a smile as she slinked away into the crowd with a conspiratorial wink toward Pen.

"Are you going to be alright?" Pen asked James, mostly for the sake of avoiding another confrontation tonight.

James eyed Savannah and Bruce as they walked away, but softened his expression as he addressed Penelope.

"Don't worry, I won't do anything to ruin your party, I think I've done enough," He said with a small, humorless smile.

"Have a glass of champagne," she offered. Out of the corner of her eye, she saw Gilda on a small stage that had been set up. She frantically gestured for Penelope to join her. "I should go before Gilda sends the cavalry."

"Go, go, I'll be fine," James said with a broader smile.

Pen briefly smiled and nodded then walked over to join Gilda, who shoved a glass of champagne into her hand. The music came to a sudden stop as soon as she was on the stage. That had a silencing effect on the crowd.

"Ladies and gentlemen, may I present the lady of the hour, one very special young lady who is celebrating her twenty-fifth birthday. Let's all raise those glasses in the air and say a cheer to Penelope Banks!"

The sound of cheering and shouts of "happy birthday" did have an elating effect on Pen's mood. Nearby, she saw that Richard had returned from handling Darren. He was standing next to Jane, Alfie, and Cousin Cordelia. Searching around, she saw Lulu still near the jazz band to the east. Benny had found a few gentlemen to keep company with further on. But they all had their glasses up in a toast to her.

Her eyes again scanned the crowd, doing a double take when she saw Lawrence among the faces. So he'd come after all. She hadn't seen him yet this evening. He grinned and winked at her, lifting his glass in salute. She flashed a brief, hesitant smile his way.

Her attention was immediately diverted by the sound of the first firework going off. Everyone turned around to watch the display of arcing lights over the water.

As she watched the show, Penelope reflected on the past year. This time last year, she had still been playing cards to make extra money, wondering if she'd make enough each weekend to help pay the rent on the apartment she had shared with Cousin Cordelia. Agnes Sterling had changed all of that. Pen was glad the last party taking place in this mansion was worthy of the woman who once owned it.

The show was fifteen minutes in when Penelope heard the scream.

It was a different pitch from the enraptured *oohs* and *ahhs* of the crowd staring up at the show lighting half of Long Island. Pen brought her attention back to the crowd to search out the source of that much more high-pitched screech of horror. She noted with relief that Lulu, Benny, Jane, Alfie, Cousin Cordelia, and Richard were still in the same spots she'd last seen them.

Then she heard another scream to the west. This time, she also heard what was being said. "Oh my God, I think he's been shot!"

CHAPTER FOURTEEN

"Did she say...he's been shot?" someone exclaimed near Penelope, she wasn't sure who. Gilda had disappeared into the crowd somewhere.

Pen felt her heart stutter then stop again, already knowing who had been shot. She caught Richard's eye before quickly descending the stage. Flashes of fireworks lit the way as she joined him down below. He took her hand and quickly headed toward the sound of the woman who was still screaming. By now it was joined with the shouts and screams of others, which were quickly beginning to replace the excited utterances at the fireworks display.

"Stand aside, please!" Richard was good at this, causing people to instantly act just from the sound of authority in his voice. They parted for him making way to the western side of the house, where Penelope had left James.

Even though she had only suspected he was the victim, it was still a shock to see James's body lying there, a circle of people around him. The nice tuxedo he had somehow conjured up, was marred only by the single blot of blood staining his white shirt.

He was dead.

"Oh, James," Pen muttered.

"James! Was it him?" That was the sound of Savannah's voice rising above the crowd as she plowed her way through. When she appeared, her face was already filled with horror. It crumpled in grief as she fell down next to James's body, picking him up to cradle him in her arms.

"No, James, please *no*!"

Richard bent down next to her and gently rested a hand on her shoulder. "Miss Duncan, I'm going to need you to let go. He's been murdered and this is now a crime scene. We want to find out who did this."

The circle around them became somber, despite the colorful display of lights in the air above and the roaring sound that accompanied them. Even that was disrupted by Bruce breaking through, from a different direction in which Savannah had appeared.

"What the hell is this? Savannah what are you doing down there? Get up you foolish girl, you're making a spectacle of yourself!" He was visibly uncomfortable under the gawking stares of everyone. Since his supposed fiancée was distraught over another man, it was understandable. He probably wasn't used to being so publicly humiliated. Or suddenly making himself one of the main suspects in a murder investigation.

Savannah lowered her head again, ignoring him as she clung to James, despite Richard's attempt to get her to let go. Pen decided to step in. She walked over and kneeled next to her, whispering in her ear.

"Savannah, come, let's go inside. Let Richard do his job, I promise he'll take care with James. The best thing we can do for him now is to find out who killed him."

THE GREAT GASTON MURDER

Savannah's eyes shot up, shooting daggers at Bruce. "*You* did this!"

His face went red with outrage. "Me? I wasn't anywhere near the damn fellow."

Pen pried Savannah's hands from James's body and stood her up, ignoring Bruce's protest.

Richard stood up as well to address the crowd again. "At the moment, everyone here is at least a witness. I'm sorry, but I have to ask everyone to stay until the police arrive. Those who were near the victim at the time of the shooting, and anyone who may have seen anything, please come forward so I can take your statements."

"I'll call the police," Pen said quietly before leading the sobbing Savannah away. She led the poor girl through the silent crowd of oglers, then inside all the way past the guard that led to Agnes's bedroom. She whispered for him to make sure to tell the other guards that no one should leave the property until the police arrived.

In the bedroom, the quiet surrounded them, now that someone outside had finally put an end to the fireworks. She set Savannah down in one of the armchairs next to the unlit fireplace. Pen took the other chair and leaned in to take her hands.

"I know this is difficult for you, Savannah. Trust me, Richard is good at his job, and I promise to put all my efforts into finding out who did this as well."

"Isn't it obvious? It was Bruce!"

"So he wasn't with you by the time the fireworks started?"

Savannah violently shook her head. "I ran away from him, trying to find James again. There were just so many—so many people, that I couldn't..." She lowered her head again, allowing her tears to come back.

Penelope gave her a moment, using the time to make the phone call to the Glen Cove Police department. Once she was connected, it was obvious that the officer on duty had not expected this kind of crime to land on his plate at this hour. She had to repeat herself several times in telling him that there had been a murder. Then, he had stuttered his way into a response, which was something along the lines of needing to contact the chief, who "wouldn't be happy about this," and call in reinforcements.

"Yes, please do. There are several hundred people here tonight. It's going to be a bit difficult to manage with only a few officers."

She hung up, hoping it wouldn't take them too long to arrive. At some point, the partiers and those working the event would start getting antsy and impatient to leave. After all, most of them were hardly suspects.

But there certainly was one man who was. Things didn't look good for Bruce. If he didn't have an alibi at the exact time of the shooting, most fingers would be pointed his way, especially after his inconsiderate outburst at finding James in Savannah's arms.

There was still Darren Combs, of course. In between attacking James, and the shooting, he'd have had time to return, gun in hand to do the dirty deed.

Who else would have had a motive?

She'd seen Lawrence Whittaker just before the fireworks started. When she had scanned the crowd just after hearing the woman scream, he had no longer been among the faces there. Where had he disappeared to?

Unfortunately, Gilda would most likely be right about this being the party of the summer. Pen doubted any of the others had involved a murder. People would be talking about it for ages, and not for anything positive.

Speaking of talking, Pen was surprised at how much she could hear, secluded in this room. Almost as though...

She stood up and walked over to the nearby window, the heavy curtains drawn for privacy. She saw the glass on the floor before she dragged the curtain aside to reveal the broken and unlatched window.

"Oh no," Penelope said, quickly rushing toward the bookcase where she had safely stored the gun Lulu had gifted her—or so she thought.

"What is it?" Savannah asked, noting how frantic Penelope was.

"It's gone!" Pen exclaimed, having pushed aside the books to discover the entire box holding the gun—and bullets!—was missing.

CHAPTER FIFTEEN

Chief Higgins himself had come out, since there were far too many people for the humble Glen Cove police department to handle. He didn't look particularly pleased to be officially on duty at this time of the morning, hours before the sun had yet to rise.

The rest of the department handled it with a mixture of irritation at being called in for duty at such an unusual hour, and fascination with the location, attendees, and circumstances. Murder was a rarity in these parts.

After hours of getting information and dismissing the party attendees, it had finally dwindled down to a manageable number, only the witnesses and those who knew James in some way remaining: Richard, Jane (and thus Alfie), Lulu, Benny, Cousin Cordelia, Savannah, Joan, Bruce, Finn, and Morris. The only missing relevant party was Lawrence Whittaker.

The police had not allowed any of the crew to clean or remove anything. That left the estate looking like a particularly morbid ghost town, the residents of which had abruptly departed before even finishing their champagne and cake. It was a sad contrast between the remaining festive touches and the gruesome circumstances. Confetti, streamers, and balloons flitted along with the sea breeze in the vast, abandoned space. The tables of food that had been picked over sat there in a sorry state from their once appetizing glory. Even the cheerful dessert area seemed a morbid sight, the colorful jars of jellybeans, gumdrops, and candy sticks, half-eaten tarts in jeweled colors, and ice cream toppings galore, all with no one to indulge. The platforms and bandstands that once showcased fire-eaters, jugglers, and the jazz band stood empty.

Penelope had, of course, rushed back to Richard after discovering her gun was missing. He hadn't been happy about it, but he'd had the decency to refrain from pointing out his earlier objections.

Chief Higgins on the other hand, hadn't held back. "So this gun of yours, you had it in your room where anyone could get at it?" He asked, giving her an incredulous look.

"No, I had a guard blocking the way to the bedroom. That's presumably why someone broke in through the window," she said, trying not to sound condescending.

He still looked put out. "And how many people knew about this gun?"

Penelope paused. That was the part where things were complicated. Really, only the people at dinner with her that night should have known about it. Then, of course, there were the two uninvited guests. She saw Richard's expression, which encouraged her to tell the truth.

"My friends, Benny, Lulu, Jane, and Detective Prescott. Then Joan and Savannah, who arrived later."

"So you flaunted this gun around at dinner?"

"No, that's when I received it. It was a gift." The last thing she wanted to do was implicate Lulu in all of this. She

THE GREAT GASTON MURDER

wouldn't have been treated with the same deference afforded to Penelope. All the more so if her loose associations with certain Irish-American gangsters were made known.

"I see," Chief Higgins said, he turned to Richard. As with most people who saw him for the first time, or as in this case, the first time in a long time, his eyes snagged on the scar to the right of his face, lingering a bit before he caught himself. "And these folks are still here, I hope?"

"Yes, I've made sure. But that doesn't preclude anyone they may have told about it. Also, we don't know for sure that it *was* the gun used in the murder. The room it was taken from is on the opposite side of the house from where the murder took place."

Pen appreciated Richard forcing Chief Higgins to be open-minded about this. He was being far more deferential than Pen was inclined to be. Her history with the chief hadn't exactly endeared him to her, and the feeling was mutual. Men had a way of respecting each other in a way they rarely afforded women.

"We'll let the experts determine if it was used or not. Now, this man who had an argument with the victim?"

"Darren Combs."

"Yes, I understand *you* escorted him away from the party?" He didn't sound too pleased with the idea that Richard had let the man go.

"Considering he had just lost his wife this week, murder apparently, I was sympathetic to his plight. I put him in one of the cars driving people back and forth to the station. He just needed a bit of drying out so he could come to his senses. He was in no condition to drive himself."

"Yes, interesting that, his wife getting murdered so close to this estate," Chief Higgins pondered, not bothering to hide his suspicion. "Do either of you have reason to believe this James Gaston was in fact the one who killed Martha Combs?"

"No, I do not," Penelope stated firmly. "He barely knew anyone in New York."

"And you know this how?"

"He told me," she said, realizing how weak that sounded as a defense. "Do *you* have reason to believe he knew her?"

He was silent for a moment, squinting one eye her way before sighing and shaking his head. "It is damn curious though."

"Perhaps it's the same person who killed James? *They* could have been the one to tell Darren that James had killed his wife. Perhaps they were hoping for just this scenario—make someone else the primary suspect as a scapegoat. Why not the husband of the deceased? It's the perfect deflection for committing the murder himself."

"Or *her*self," the Chief said pointedly.

"Yes, or herself," Penelope said testily, even though he did have a point. If her gun was used in this murder, after ruling out her friends whom she'd seen by the time the murder had happened, the only other people who would have known about it were female. "All the same, I think it behooves you to interview Darren Combs and find out who told him about his wife. They might be the suspect."

"Thank you, Miss Banks, I'll be sure to do that now that you've suggested it," he said, his voice filled with sarcasm. Even Richard gave her an exasperated look.

"I apologize for my tone. Of course, I wouldn't deign to tell you how to do your job. This has all just been so trying. Two murders, one of whom was my own guest," she said, making sure to add a thick layer of feminine distress to her

THE GREAT GASTON MURDER

voice. In reality, she was still shaken up and saddened by James's murder, so it wasn't that difficult.

Chief Higgins knew Penelope too well to be so gullible. "Yes, two murders the same week you decide to grace us with your presence...yet again. You seem to carry an awful lot of bad luck where you go, Miss Banks. At least for those around you."

"Agnes's murder happened before I arrived," she reminded him.

"Yes, yes," he said dismissing it. "Let's get to you explaining how you knew this victim, James Gaston."

"He was really a guest of Agnes's." At the way he arched an eyebrow in confusion, she explained. "She had been his patron, he was an artist. She's the one who sent him to Paris to study art. He returned this past Saturday, or so he said."

"So he was here during the murder of Martha Combs?"

"But he didn't have a car, as far as I know. One of your officers already talked to him."

"Yes, I talked with the officer," Chief Higgins said, stroking his chin in thought. "And you still have no idea what Mrs. Combs may have been doing in this part of Long Island? It is quite the coincidence."

"Yes, a coincidence. Did you happen to follow up on the jellybean I called about?"

"Jellybean?"

"I found a pink jellybean on the side of the road near where Martha Combs was killed. I thought it might have some relevance. I called and told one of your officers about it."

"No, Miss Banks, we did not follow up on any jellybean," he said, as though she were playing a prank on him.

"But for now, let's focus on the murder of James Gaston, shall we?"

Richard gave her a subtle shake of the head, telling her to just comply. She was in no mood for an argument—there would be plenty of time for finger wagging later—so she sighed and let it go. No doubt summers took the heaviest toll on Chief Higgins's department even on a good day, what with New Yorkers flocking in droves to the shores of Long Island. Now this, and so close to the end of summer.

"There is someone else you should look into, a Lawrence Whittaker," she said, figuring at least this might have been a more helpful lead. "He told me he was James's agent. He was here tonight. Yesterday he came by to see James and I overheard the two of them having an argument." She told him about Mr. Whittaker's arrival and the argument she'd overheard.

"And he's gone?" Chief Higgins asked in a rather accusatory tone, making sure to cast a quick, irritated glance Richard's way.

"He disappeared into the crowd just before the murder took place," Penelope said. She refrained from adding the rather impertinent bit that if she had known James was to be murdered she would have kept better track of the man.

He nodded with a disgruntled look on his face. "I'll check with the officers, see if they caught anyone by that name."

Penelope had an idea that they most certainly would not have. Mr. Whittaker seemed like the wily sort. If he *was* the murderer, he would have escaped long before the police came.

They were just then interrupted by a policeman who came upon them, breathless from his eagerness to report the news.

THE GREAT GASTON MURDER

"We found the gun and the box!"

"Good," Chief Higgins said with a firm nod. He turned back to Penelope. "You stay right here."

"Perhaps she should accompany us, Chief Higgins. Miss Banks would best be able to identify the gun and the box, don't you think?" Richard suggested.

Penelope was grateful to him for that. He was subtly making sure she was included in this. He could have easily identified the gun and box himself. Chief Higgins wouldn't have known he was there when it was first gifted to her.

"Yes, and I'm hardly a suspect, am I?" Pen added. "Nearly a hundred people could confirm that I was on the stage before James was found shot."

Chief Higgins didn't seem pleased, but he nodded all the same. Penelope followed them outside. They went through the front doors and turned west, which made sense as James was killed near the west wing of the house. The officer quickly stomped his way across the lawn, which had already suffered enough abuse during the party, and came to a stop about twenty yards away from where James's body was. He had thankfully already been taken away.

Lying right there was her gun, complete with the jade inlay. They all stared at Pen with expectant looks.

"Yes, that is my gun. Is it loaded?"

"It is not," the officer confirmed. "But it has been fired. The smell of gunpowder is still there."

"Which means at one point recently there was a bullet in the chamber that was indeed fired. All it takes is one, Miss Banks," Chief Higgins said, once again giving her a look of disapproval as though this was all her fault.

"I see," she said with a sigh. It was looking more and more likely that her gun had in fact been used to commit the crime. "You said that you also found the box that it was in?"

"We did," he said, gesturing in the opposite direction. They all followed the officer back to the east side of the house near the wing where Agnes's bedroom was located. It made sense that the thief would have dropped the box here, rather than carry such a cumbersome load all the way to the scene of the murder. Whereas the gun was small enough that it could have easily been hidden in a pocket, a purse, or underneath a jacket, the box was not.

"Right here," the officer said as they approached another policeman standing guard over a shiny black box not too far from the broken, open window of Agnes's bedroom.

"Yes, that is the missing box as well. If you check, there's a small button you press to open a side drawer. There should be six bullets there, though I suppose that might be five now."

Chief Higgins did the honors himself, pulling out a handkerchief to press where Penelope pointed. The box popped open, revealing...only five bullets.

"That's enough for me to work under the assumption that your gun was used, Miss Banks. At least until the evidence reveals otherwise. The only question now is, who knew about this gun, specifically where you had it tucked away during the party?"

"With all due respect, Chief Higgins, aren't we getting a little ahead of ourselves here?" Richard protested. "It shouldn't take long to at least retrieve the bullet. It may be intact enough to compare it to those still in the box to give you something more definitive than this circumstantial evidence."

"Also, shouldn't you also check for fingerprints?" Pen said.

Once again, Chief Higgins met them with irritation and

THE GREAT GASTON MURDER

disdain. "Yes, of course, we plan on doing our due diligence. We'll check the bullet in the victim. And obviously, we'll get fingerprints to at least make a determination of who touched the box and the gun. Glen Cove may not be as *advanced* as the Manhattan police departments, but we aren't a bunch of backwoods hicks either."

"Of course, I would never imply as much," Richard said respectfully.

"As for you, Miss Banks, I think we have all we need from you. Officer Thayer will escort you back to the library. We'll have someone down to take fingerprints of everyone, including you—just for elimination purposes of course," he said with a dry smile. Richard gave a subtle nod, as though she should just comply without protest.

As though Pen would let that stop her. "Did you know I've become a private investigator since we last met, Chief Higgins? As Detective Prescott can confirm, I've helped solve quite a few murder cases this past year." Certainly more than the Glen Cove police department would have, seeing how rare crime was in that wealthy enclave of Long Island. "I would be more than happy to lend my services in this case."

The chief met her with a patronizing smile that already told her his thoughts on that idea. "I think we in the Glen Cove police department will be just fine without your help, young lady."

Pen felt her mouth tighten with irritation at being so casually and patronizingly dismissed. Still, she hadn't done herself any favors, knowing how prickly the chief was when it came to her, in particular, telling him how to do his job. Richard, of course, could get away with it.

"Again, Officer Thayer will escort you back to the library."

"Actually, chief, I'll escort Miss Banks back," Richard gave her an amused look. "She has a habit of wriggling her way out of the clutches of police officers."

Pen wasn't in the least amused. All the more so since the last time she had wriggled her way out of the clutches of police officers, she had inadvertently helped solve Agnes's murder. She scowled as she followed him back toward the front of the house.

"If I'd known how easily your loyalties were diverted, I would have thought twice about letting you kiss me on that roof. Or spend so much time in my quarters while you were here."

"Hmm, I seem to recall you being quite the willing participant in each of those...endeavors."

"Don't you dare use that word right now," Penelope snapped, feeling her temperature rise even more. The word certainly had an amusing history between the two of them, but Penelope was in no mood to be flirtatious or coy.

"My apologies, Miss Banks."

"Don't you dare call me that either," she said, feeling petty and irate. He was deliberately winding her up in the hopes that she'd be less difficult. It was having entirely the opposite effect.

Pen stopped walking and spun around to face him. "I'm just as good a detective as you are."

"Of course," he said in a serious tone.

"I could actually contribute something valuable to this case."

"Yes, of course."

"I've solved more murders than that pompous...incorrigible...buffoon!"

"Absolutely."

THE GREAT GASTON MURDER

"You're teasing me!" Pen snapped, realizing what he was doing in that oh-so-serious voice of his.

"I'm waiting for you to finish, calm down, and give me a chance to explain my idea?" He hinted. "Something that will help this case and soothe your wounded pride."

Penelope glared.

"Have you exhausted your outrage?"

"Keep patronizing me and I think you'll find a resurgence."

"Fair point. Now, I think perhaps you could in fact be useful in your capacity as a private investigator...in the library."

She crossed her arms and frowned.

"Where almost all of the suspects are still waiting?"

He was making a good point, an excellent point, in fact. She still waved back toward where Chief Higgins was. "Yes, but—"

"And you know I'll tell you as much as I can from what I learn out here among the officers and the chief. Doesn't that make the most sense?"

"Yes, I suppose...*Detective Prescott.*"

"Don't think of this as some lesser treatment because you're a woman, Penelope," he said, guiding her along back into the house again. "Besides, you did know the victim after all."

"I only met him this week!"

"And you're not a police officer."

"So, you don't think my being a woman has *anything* to do with it?" Pen protested.

"Of course it does, but I believe you were the one to once reveal to me that you catch more flies with honey? Heaven knows I've seen you use your womanly wiles to get your way before."

127

"Don't turn that against me. We all use what weapons we have in our arsenal," she scoffed, feeling a begrudging smile come to her face. "It's certainly worked on you."

"It certainly has," he said with a grin.

Penelope snapped her head around to look at him in surprise.

"What?" Richard said, still staring forward with a grin as they walked. "Do you think I'm that gullible? You should be flattered, even when I know you're manipulating me, I still fall for it. Or at least allow you to think I am."

Penelope smiled, unable to hold her grudge against him or even the circumstances. Besides, his plan made sense. While he worked with the police department outside, she would find out what she could from the people in the library. If anything, her skills were better put to use there.

He walked her as far as the entrance to the library, gave her one last encouraging look, and then left.

"Well, what did they find?" Bruce demanded.

"My gun, and the box it came in," Penelope said. "It seems it may have been the murder weapon."

CHAPTER SIXTEEN

The sun had officially risen in the sky, casting a deceptively cheerful shine on the day. The people who had been kept behind after James's murder were occupying the library of the mansion, still in their party clothes. Savannah was safely huddled between Cousin Cordelia and Jane, who had Alfie on her other side. Pen's cousin was suddenly more distraught than even Savannah.

"What is this about you having a gun, Penelope?" Cousin Cordelia asked in horror. As though the day needed any more dramatics.

Pen sighed inwardly. Cousin Cordelia hadn't been there when Lulu had given her the present. Now, she would have to detour from her original plan to find out who had stolen it in order to explain.

"I was gifted a gun for my birthday, Cousin. Last night someone stole it. It may have been used in this crime."

"Oh!" Cousin Cordelia looked as though she might faint. Now, it was Savannah turning to place an arm around her in comfort. Jane quickly rose and came around to her other side.

"So, it would seem your twenty-fifth year is getting off to a galloping start," Benny said with a wry smile. "All that's missing is the champagne."

"The last thing we need is more ammunition for the police," Lulu said in a decidedly less tickled tone, sitting next to him. It took a lot to unsettle or worry a woman like her, considering the world she operated in, but Pen could see the hint of it in her eyes. She walked over to sit next to her and reassuringly squeezed her hand.

"Don't worry, I can confirm you didn't shoot James," she said confidentially. "At the time of the murder, I saw you as well as Benny, Jane and Alfie, and Cousin Cordelia. I'll swear to it on a Bible."

"Let's hope that's good enough."

"Lulu, you give me too little credit," Pen whispered with a sly look. "I am a private investigator after all. Besides, we don't know for sure that the gun was used in the crime."

She ignored both skeptical looks Benny and Lulu gave her. Instead, focusing on the only two other people in the room who may have stolen that gun.

"It *is* rather odd that my gun would be stolen around the same time the murder took place," she said loudly enough for everyone to hear.

To her surprise, Joan threw back her head and laughed. "Oh Penelope, at least Sherlock Holmes would have come right out and accused me of the crime. It was that lovely little gun of yours that was used, was it not?"

"So it would seem," Pen said, letting the insult pass.

"My, my, that does put an interesting twist on things. How many people actually knew about the gun? Not very many. Really only those at the little dinner of yours Savie and I crashed, no?" She made sure to shoot Bruce a devilish grin.

THE GREAT GASTON MURDER

"Knowing you, I wouldn't be surprised if you stole it and killed him just to amuse yourself," Bruce spat.

"Hmm, my cousin does have a point, I do so live for the thrill. We all know sweet Savannah wouldn't have killed him, which leaves yours truly as the only other party who knew about the gun. It must have been me. How convenient that my prints were already on the gun. Brava, yet again Penelope, you've solved the case!"

"Stop lying, Joan," Savannah said, suddenly alert with intensity. She directed her attention to Bruce with a baleful look. "Joan told Bruce about the gun. I was there when she did. It was when those three got back from another boating trip. She told them all about it, even where you were hiding it."

Pen turned to give Joan an exasperated look. She still had a grin on her face as she shrugged apologetically. "Ah yes, that little fact must have slipped my mind. Guilty as charged, I suppose! It was just too delicious not to tell."

"Meddlesome as ever, Joan," Morris said, giving her a dark look.

"We all know why you *really* told," Savannah said, glaring at her.

Yes, it did seem like Joan enjoyed being a fly in the ointment. She probably relished the idea of Bruce finding out that his betrothed was visiting a former paramour late at night, and used the gun as an excuse.

"That doesn't mean I used your stupid gun to kill anyone," Bruce protested. "Besides, I have my own guns. Almost all of you have seen my collection right here in Long Island! I certainly wouldn't need to borrow some silly little jade thing if I wanted to kill a man."

"So you *have* seen it then," Penelope accused.

"What?"

"How would you have known the gun had a jade handle if you hadn't?"

"Admittedly, I did tell him about that little detail as well. How could I not? It was the most interesting bit," Joan said, again with a smile that belied her guilty shrug.

"That still proves nothing," Bruce snapped.

Pen could see how uncomfortable he was, which was understandable. He was no doubt replaying his earlier outburst in his head and kicking himself. Out of everyone in the room, he was the most likely suspect in killing James. He would have been even without the scene he'd made. In fact, if anything, that made him somewhat *less* likely to be the suspect. It would have been incredibly stupid to kill a man right after revealing to the world that you knew about your fiancée's feelings toward him. Then again, Bruce wasn't exactly the ripest apple in the barrel.

"You're right it doesn't prove anything, Bruce. They have nothing on you. And if they're fingerprinting everyone, then it will only prove your innocence," Morris said, giving him a questioning look.

"They won't find my fingerprints on any damn jade gun," Bruce insisted.

Morris nodded, then turned to give Penelope a satisfied look.

"This is an outrage," Finn exclaimed, throwing his hands up in protest. "I don't see why we have to stay here. They haven't arrested us. Surely any interrogations or fingerprints that need to be taken can be handled at a later time? This is really quite trying. My sister is understandably distraught. She needs to be resting in bed, not held here like some criminal."

"I'm quite fine," Savannah said with surprising venom

as she glared at him. "If it means finding out who killed James, then I'll stay here all day."

"Since *I* haven't killed anyone, I'm going to put my foot down on the matter," Bruce said testily. He strutted toward the door of the library and stormed out. Morris and Finn were right behind him.

Penelope watched them go in surprise before springing into action to follow them. "You can't leave before fingerprints are taken," she insisted as they blazed into the foyer, startling the two officers already there.

"Woah, woah," said one, his hands held up in protest. "Where do you think you're going? You can't leave just yet, sir."

Outside there was suddenly additional commotion. It distracted the officers just enough that the three men were able to continue on. The policemen and Penelope had no choice but to follow. In the driveway, she saw two officers dragging a struggling Darren Combs from the back of their car. He was still dressed as he had been last night when he confronted James, though this morning he looked perfectly disheveled—and still quite ossified.

"We caught him wandering down Brookline Drive looking for where his wife was killed. Wasn't even on the right stretch of road! He's been here in Glen Cove the whole damn time."

CHAPTER SEVENTEEN

Chief Higgins and Richard were already approaching the two officers who had Darren Combs in a vice grip between them. He looked perfectly defeated, his head hanging down as though he'd given up on life already.

"Well, it would seem your attempts to send Mr. Combs on his way didn't go according to plan, Detective Prescott," Chief Higgins said with a mixture of satisfaction and condemnation.

Penelope remained on the front steps standing next to Finn, Morris, and Bruce. The latter looked even more pleased than the chief did at this new development.

"There now, that solves that," Finn said, looking more relieved than anyone. He was no doubt grateful that the nuptials for his sister no longer faced the not-so-minor obstacle of a murder trial.

"So much for placing the blame on Bruce," Morris said giving Pen a smirk.

"Need I remind you that someone has died? *Two* people in fact, one of whom was your own maid, Morris?"

"And I shall have a drink in both their honors—back at my own home. I'm sure the chief will be more accommodating about our departure now that they've caught the obvious suspect."

"You three seem awfully eager to leave, conveniently before they've even taken fingerprints," Pen hinted.

"There's no need to waste the valuable time of upstanding members of society with that banana oil," Bruce groused. "We aren't common criminals, after all, we deserve a certain amount of deference. And being held here against our will is an outrage. In fact, I have it in mind to—"

"None of you are going anywhere until you've been fingerprinted," Richard said, casually approaching them, having heard their exchange. He spoke calmly but firmly. "Unless you want the police coming to your homes to do it. And I guarantee if we're forced to do that, then we'll be coming with search warrants and tearing apart every inch of your life as we do so."

Penelope shot him a subtle smile, hoping the others didn't notice it. She enjoyed this rather commanding side of him. It certainly shut up the lofty trio next to her.

Bruce eyed the tuxedo Richard was still wearing and narrowed his eyes. "And just who are you? Certainly not a police officer."

"Detective Richard Prescott," he said, leaving off the part about working out of the 10A precinct in Manhattan, which was decidedly out of the Glen Cove jurisdiction. "So, what'll be, boys? Are you going to cooperate, or do you prefer taking your chances with us discovering evidence of certain, ah, vices in your homes?"

"Fine, let's get this over with," Morris snapped, turning to the other two. "It's fingerprints, nothing too intrusive. If they want anything more, we can call our attorneys."

"Indeed," Richard said.

"I don't see why we even need to be that accommodating," Finn scoffed.

"Because I don't want the police tearing through my home, Finn," Bruce gritted out, giving his future brother-in-law a look that cowed him into submission.

"The wisest decision," Richard said. Before he could say anything more, Chief Higgins called him over to where they were still holding Darren Combs.

"Poor sap," Morris muttered. "I get being mad enough to finally snap when it came to Martha. She certainly enjoyed flaunting her flings in his face. But to kill James so publicly. I doubt they'll even bother with a trial."

"There's no proof he killed James, or his own wife for that matter," Penelope said, then turned her steely gaze to Morris. "After all, I doubt they'll find *his* prints on the gun either. How would he have even known about it?" None of the three had anything to say to that.

The police officers were squirreling Darren back into the car. Chief Higgins was speaking to Richard and they both nodded in agreement before the latter came back to the front steps of the house.

Richard guided Penelope away, out of earshot of the others. "They're taking him to the station. I'm going to go with them as a courtesy to participate in the interview."

"What about the fingerprints?"

"They're still sending someone out to get them, also as a courtesy. I don't think he wants anyone here crowding his station just to handle that business."

"Remind him that he is going to find my fingerprints as well as Lulu's and Joan's."

"Of course."

"I can't believe my own gun was used for this."

"We still don't know that."

Penelope gave him a sardonic look.

He smiled back. "I feel like our roles are reversed this time around. Usually, you're the one playing devil's advocate."

Penelope breathed out a soft laugh, which quickly faded. "If it wasn't my gun, that means it's all the more likely it was Darren Combs."

"Perhaps."

"I assume they'd didn't find a smoking gun on him?"

"No, but there are a number of places he could have discarded it. I suppose he stopped the car last night when he realized he was on the road where his wife was killed."

"Yet another murder to solve. I hope they aren't diverting resources away from Martha's murder for this."

"They may be connected."

"How?" Penelope asked, her brow wrinkling in thought. Granted, there was a fair amount of interconnectedness between Martha and James. The three men standing on the front steps, now looking their way with wary regard, certainly had some connection to one or both of the victims. So did two of the women still in the library.

"Tell Chief Higgins to hurry with the fingerprinting. I don't know how much longer these people are going to play nice."

"Will do. In the meantime..."

"I shall be doing my own bit of investigating," Pen said with a conspiratorial smile.

Penelope watched him as he headed back to the car to join Chief Higgins and one of the other officers who sat in the back with Darren.

"Well Pen, I realize I have yet to wish you a happy twenty-fifth birthday," Bruce called out with not so much of a hint of goodwill. "Instead, allow me to wish you a year of nothing but misfortune and troubles."

Pen's mouth fell open. "That's a perfectly cruel thing to say, Bruce. Even for you."

Both Finn and Morris also looked taken aback, but at this point, they weren't likely to side with Penelope.

"I think you'll find I can be more than cruel, Pen. If you think worms down the back of your dress was a mean prank, wait until you see what I'm capable of as an adult. I won't have the Carlton family name, or those who will soon be joined with us sullied by ties to this tasteless murder business."

"I suppose if the victims knew what an inconvenience it would be for you, they would have avoided getting themselves killed."

"If only," he said without an ounce of sarcasm. "I'm going back inside to await this fingerprinting mess, then I'm collecting Savannah and we're leaving."

He stormed back inside. Finn lingered to give her an uncertain look, as though he was unsure whether he should offer some balm to soothe the harsh words. In the end, he said nothing, and followed Bruce inside.

Morris did the opposite. He smiled and strolled over to her side. "Don't take his words to heart, Penelope. You know Bruce, he's always been a bit of a bully. He doesn't mean what he says."

"You and I both know that's not true. Still, heaven help me if simple words are enough to affect me at this point. I got quite an earful of the things you and the old set said about me the past three years."

He pursed his lips with mock offense.

"Did Bruce know about Savannah and James? I mean before we both came to visit that day? Joan mentioned he had a telescope through which one could see the grounds here. Perhaps he accidentally happened upon them one night?"

"I suppose it's a possibility. He does like to, *ahem*, enjoy all that Mother Nature has to offer through that thing often enough," Morris said with a wicked grin.

"He's such a despicable cad," Penelope muttered with disdain. She shouldn't have been surprised that Bruce was that kind of degenerate, hoping to spy on a woman in an indelicate moment.

"Oh stop, Pen, every home in Sands Point has one. Even my home does, not that I use it for such unsavory purposes," he said with mock indignation. "Then again, Bruce has never been a saint. I don't blame Savannah for anything she's done. What is it she and James claimed they've been up to? No doubt a harmless bit of painting? Perhaps another canvas for the sitting room, with which to taunt poor Bruce," he said with a laugh. "The artist painting his subject on the porch by the light of the silvery moon," he crooned with an eyebrow devilishly arched. "Really, it's all so cliché."

"So is murdering someone out of jealousy. Cliché enough to make Bruce the primary suspect, despite Darren's arrest. Honestly, I'm surprised he's being so accommodating about the fingerprinting."

Morris's grin faded. "Most likely because he knows he never touched that gun."

"Or he's even more worried about his home being searched?"

"Keep pushing, Penelope. You may find that his threats are not so idle."

"And you? You don't seem all that bothered that your

family has lost a maid to murder and now perhaps a chauffeur to a murder charge?"

"Maids and chauffeurs can be replaced." He came in closer and gave her a challenging look. "Has it occurred to you that perhaps Martha was here visiting your friend James that night? That perhaps Savannah wasn't the only woman he had ideas on? That perhaps he didn't like how things ended with Martha? That perhaps Darren had very good reason to threaten him?"

"Were you the one that told him his wife may have been involved with James? Suggested that this might be why he killed her?"

Morris paused before answering. "I simply presented the facts to him. She was in Long Island when she shouldn't have been, she was in Glen Cove, for some *odd* reason. And James, the handsome stranger, just so happened to be here at the same time."

"He didn't suspect you at all?"

Morris chuckled and shook his head. "Nice try, Pen. But to answer your question, no. My tastes are a little bit loftier than the hired help. Martha was problematic enough, always rifling around in places she didn't belong and pretending she didn't know any better. Besides, my parents aren't the type to endure that kind of upstairs-downstairs drama in their own household. We're all very much kept on a short leash, aren't we?" he said bitterly. "You should know better than anyone."

Pen ignored that. "Still, you know she cheated, you must know with whom?"

"And if I'm ever put under oath I shall spill it all. Until then, I'll leave it at that. Still, Darren put up with it all the same. Though it would seem he apparently drew the line at someone murdering her. Is it any wonder he made such a ruckus?"

Penelope stared at him, appalled. Morris may very well have been the cause of James's death and he seemed to feel no guilt about it whatsoever. The callous way some of the wealthy treated those they thought inferior to them often amazed her, even after having grown up in that world.

"Happy Birthday, Pen." Morris cocked his mouth into a lopsided smile before strolling back inside.

At this point, Penelope almost hoped it was either Bruce, Morris, or Finn who had committed these murders, if only to rip them from their lofty pedestals with the humiliation of a public murder trial. And of course to save Darren an even worse fate of spending the rest of his life in prison. Frankly, the three of them were giving her no reason to believe they were entirely innocent.

CHAPTER EIGHTEEN

The officer doing the fingerprinting had come and gone. Penelope had made sure to tell him about the three women whose fingerprints might be found on the murder weapon and the box, even though she was certain Richard would remind him of it back at the station.

Bruce, Finn, and Morris had been all too willing to give their prints, which meant either they hadn't used the gun to kill James, or, if they had, they had made sure not to touch anything directly.

"We're going, now," Bruce said looking perfectly indignant. "This has been an outrage. Frankly, I have it in mind to get my parents involved, perhaps have a word with the mayor or whoever runs this damn municipality."

Penelope ignored him, quite fatigued with his histrionics. It was bad enough that someone had thought to bring Cousin Cordelia a glass and a bottle of brandy, the latter of which she had squirreled away behind a pillow, though not without taking a few nips here and there.

Morris and Finn followed Bruce as far as the doorway to

the library but stopped when he did, turning back to note that Savannah hadn't so much as budged.

"Well, are you coming, Savannah?" Finn demanded.

"I don't think so," she said in a calm voice. She turned to Penelope. "If you don't mind, I—I'd rather not leave."

"Of course. I can have Chives prepare a room for you."

"Do you suppose I could stay in James's cottage?"

Bruce coughed with incredulity. "I beg your pardon?"

"Actually, I believe the police have prohibited any of us from entering. They consider it relevant to the murder for now."

Savannah's eyes widened briefly, then lowered with sorrow once again. She silently nodded in understanding.

"But that doesn't mean you can't still stay here."

"She most certainly will not!" Bruce raged. "Just because your own wedding failed, doesn't give you the right to interfere in others' Penelope. My fiancée is coming with me, now!"

He stormed over, as though he intended to snatch her from the couch and drag her back home. Jane gasped, Cousin Cordelia wailed in terror, but Alfie was the one to step in to intercede.

With quick agility, he stood up and blocked his way. Alfie was incredibly tall, but it wasn't his height that cowed Bruce into stopping, it was his oddly serene bearing. He gently placed a hand on his chest and stared unwaveringly with those delightful eyes of his from behind his glasses.

"I think it best that you leave without any further disturbances. The police already have their hands full with two murders, there is no reason they should divert their efforts with attempted kidnapping."

"Kidnapping? She's to be my wife!"

"The operative words are 'to be.' And it seems

your *future* wife has made her desires known. On the other hand, it doesn't seem as though you have endeared yourself to the local police department. As Miss Banks's friend is also a member of law enforcement, I'm sure he would have no problem fitting you into a charge of kidnapping if only to have you constrained while they focus on more important work."

"Alfred is to be an attorney specializing in criminal law, Bruce. I suggest you heed his wisdom." Penelope couldn't help the bit of taunt that colored her voice. Like Jane, who stared up at him with naked awe and admiration, she was rather impressed by his interference.

Bruce's mouth opened and closed like a fish out of water, before he went red and spun around to storm out. Finn shot daggers toward his sister before following. Morris simply looked slightly amused by the whole display before casually following them.

"It would seem Joan is once again the forgotten cousin," Joan said from her perch on the window sill. "Do I stay and mourn? Or tag along with Bruce to drink and rage? Decisions, decisions..."

"You of course are welcome to stay as well," Penelope said tiredly. Frankly, despite what she had told Savannah, at this point they would have to make use of the other cottages on the property. Especially if Alfred stayed. She doubted Jane was as libertine when it came to sharing bedrooms as Richard and she were. On top of this, Agnes's room was now also part of a crime scene.

"Then that settles it! I shall stay," Joan announced.

Savannah sighed and closed her eyes with dismay. Her attention was quickly corralled by Cousin Cordelia having a brandy-fueled fit.

"Oh, this is just too much, too much indeed! Two

murders, in the very house where poor Agnes met her tragic end. There was a second murder back then as well, do you remember Penelope? It's bound to happen to one of us. A murderer right here under the same roof once again! We shall all be killed in our sleep, I'm sure of it!"

Savannah and Jane both put their arm around her cousin, trying to comfort her.

"Perhaps I should take her back to her room now that the police are done with us?" Jane offered.

"I think that would be a good idea," Pen said, trying to mask her relief.

They got up to leave, Jane gently releasing the bottle of brandy from Cousin Cordelia's hand that she still had a firm grip on, before guiding her out. Savannah was left alone on the sofa, realizing that all eyes were on her. Pen walked over to sit next to her.

"I apologize for my cousin. Usually, she limits her intake to a nip or two in the morning. Her medicine, she calls it. In all fairness, she did have a prescription once upon a time."

"You mean to tell me that's who you've been buying all those little flasks for?" Lulu asked with a wry smile from the couch opposite them. She had been Pen's source for Cousin Cordelia's bootleg "medicinal" brandy for the past few years now, unbeknownst to the poor woman.

"You can see why we so often run out. Again, she usually isn't this bad, but murder does tend to try her delicate constitution."

"It's quite alright," Savannah said. "I understand how this might be trying for everyone. At least she allowed me to forget about James for a moment." That seemed to bring back the understanding that he was dead, murdered in fact. Her face wrinkled with grief again.

"Are there any other family or friends you have here in New York?"

A sad smile came to her face and she shook her head. "I haven't really been allowed an opportunity to make my own friends. All my friends are Bruce's. He keeps a close eye on what I do and where I go, at least when he isn't out... indulging in his own activities," she added bitterly.

So Savannah was aware of him stepping out on her. A soft, nervous laugh escaped Savannah's lips and she grabbed her purse. She dug into it and pulled out a handful of jellybeans—pink jellybeans. Exactly like the one Pen had found where Martha had been killed.

Penelope stared down at them in surprise. Savannah misread her reaction.

"Sorry, I grabbed a handful from one of the jars outside. It's my favorite flavor. I eat them when I get nervous or upset, as the sugar calms me. I really shouldn't, of course. I used to sneak these as a little girl. Mama always forbade me any sweets. 'Mustn't get too fat!' Bruce seemed just as fond of that rule, always belittling me when I had dessert or a piece of chocolate."

He really was a bully. No wonder Savannah was so distraught that the man she hoped to escape with was now dead. James would probably have been the sort of husband to buy them for her just because he knew they were her favorite.

He'd also be the kind of loyal beau to try and dissuade Penelope from calling the police to let them know about a pink jellybean near a murder scene. Pen had assumed he was simply distrustful of the police and wanted to avoid them as much as possible. Now, it seemed there may have been another motive: he wanted to protect Savannah.

"I enjoyed sneaking in a trip to Marcell's Candy Shop

when Bruce thought I was shopping in Manhattan," she continued, unaware that Pen was studying her in a different light. "Dresses, hats, gloves, and shoes are fine to spend his family's money on, but he would have thrown a fit if he knew I spent twenty-five cents on a bag of jellybeans."

"So you carry them with you often?" Pen asked, hoping she didn't sound too accusatory.

"Often enough. I have a stash hidden back at home —*his* home," she said with a frown. "I know he's found them in my dresser. I suspect he's been going through my closets and drawers. I have no privacy whatsoever. I had to hide all my letters from James under the mattress."

"I can see why you wanted to stay here. And you're welcome as long as you like," Pen said honestly. All the better to discover if Savannah had been the one to kill Martha Combs.

CHAPTER NINETEEN

Penelope could hardly contain herself long enough for Richard to return. The police were still mulling about, studiously ignoring the copious amounts of half-filled bottles of alcohol that still remained. Penelope suspected that at least a few of them would go missing by the time this mess was over. That was fine by her, perhaps they deserved it for being snatched into service at such a rude hour.

The police had allowed her back into Agnes's room long enough to change her clothes, since she had still been in her party dress, which looked the worse for wear. Now, she was in a far more sensible frock that had a less festive flair to it.

When Richard did return, she flew to him, not bothering to wait and see what he had to say about Darren Combs. He'd been gone a good hour.

"He didn't confess did he?" Pen asked, just to make sure her planned excursion wasn't pointless.

"No, he keeps insisting he just wanted to punch James, rough him up a bit. Claims he doesn't even own a gun. Then, when he finally sobered up a bit, he asked for his attorney and refused to answer any more questions. They're holding him on assault and drunk and disorderly charges."

"Then, we need to go to the Carlton home. Quickly!"

"I take it you learned something interesting," he said wryly, a calm front against Penelope's storm of impatience.

"I've discovered a clue and I need to make sure it leads to something before we tell Chief Higgins. Come, come!" She took him by the hand and dragged him back to his car.

"Am I allowed to at least change out of my tuxedo first?" He gestured to his clothes. He'd only managed to undo his bowtie.

"No time for that. Besides, you look too dashing and handsome to change." He did not appear to be moved by her flattery, but went along with her anyway.

"So, what is it you discovered?" Richard asked as they drove off.

"Savannah was eating pink jellybeans."

"Well, case closed then."

"Don't be smart. It's evidence. When Leonard was driving James and me back from the Carltons' home, I had him stop so I could do a little investigating, as is my profession," Pen said, being rather smart herself.

"So it is."

"*Stop the car!*" Pen said suddenly. For the second time, she had the driver of a car skidding to a stop on Brookline Drive. Richard turned to give her the same exasperated look Leonard had.

"This is where I found it," Penelope explained, pointing ahead. She jumped out of the car and walked further down to the exact spot where her peculiar memory remembered finding the stain. "Hmm, the rain must have washed it away. But this is where Martha was killed."

She trailed her way back toward the brush by the side of

the road where she'd seen the pink jellybean. Richard followed her.

"The jellybean was right here, I'm certain of—oh." Pen stopped, wrinkling her nose when she found the candy, or what was left of it. The ants had finally discovered it and had made fine work of chewing it apart so that it was barely recognizable.

"I suppose that could have once been considered a jellybean," Richard said with a frown.

"I wasn't certain whether it was evidence or not at the time. Also, I thought it best not to touch it just in case. I did call the police department and tell them about it. Obviously, they didn't take my information seriously. Now, look at it!"

Richard stared at the jellybean then turned to look further down the road where Pen had said Martha was killed. "I wouldn't be too harsh on them. What would Mrs. Combs have been doing over here in the brush so far from where she was run over?"

"Perhaps she got out, or was pushed out? Perhaps Savannah chased her and tackled her to the ground, then got in the car and ran her over."

"There's an image. But let's not assume Savannah is guilty based on a piece of candy."

"This candy may very well be the key to everything." Pen stared down at it again. "That's if there's anything left before the ants finish with it," she hinted.

Richard sighed heavily then winced. "I suppose I'll have to be the one to pick it up."

"It would be the gentlemanly thing to do," Penelope said tartly. "Also, as you were so quick to remind me, I'm not an official member of law enforcement."

He breathed out a soft laugh before pulling out his handkerchief and gingerly plucking up what remained of the pink candy. He shook off as many of the ants as he could before flicking the more stubborn ones away with his finger.

"So, we have a single pink jellybean about," he squinted down the road, "ten yards away from where Mrs. Combs was murdered?"

"Correct," Pen said, eager to get going again. "Now that we have the jellybean, we need to check the cars at Bruce's home for any sign that they were used in the accident."

Richard put the handkerchief-wrapped candy in his pocket and followed Pen back to the car.

"Did Darren have any idea why his wife was in Long Island? Apparently, she was supposed to be back in Manhattan. Better yet, did he know what she was doing out here in Glen Cove?" Penelope asked when he started off again.

"He was a bit coy on that front. While he was still in his cups, he waxed on about how unhappy she seemed to be with her lot in life. He'd gotten her the job with the Belmonts, but it only made her resentful of their lowly circumstances, and him by comparison. I suppose no man wants to come out and admit that his wife has been stepping out on him, but that's the impression I got. He couldn't tell me any names though."

"If she was looking to tie herself to someone who could have her nicely heeled, there are plenty of candidates, especially here. Long Island is infested with the idle rich during the summer. The Belmonts associate mostly with other people from Old Money. Someone living in Glen Cove would have been a rare visitor to their home, though I suppose it's not impossible to find a connection. I'm just trying to piece that together with Savannah and that darn jellybean. If she knew Bruce was involved with Martha, I don't think she'd be jealous enough to kill her. She wanted to be with James, after all. I also can't figure out why she'd bring her all the way out here to do the deed. All it does is have the police poking around in this area where James was staying."

"One thing at a time. If we find any evidence on one of the cars from the Carlton home then we can move forward with questioning her." They arrived at the home, Penelope giving Richard directions.

"Is it supposed to resemble a castle?" Richard asked, scrutinizing the home with an unimpressed frown.

"I think that was the idea."

"It looks more like some prisons I've seen."

"My thoughts exactly. But there's a car here in the driveway. That means at least someone is home. Are you allowed to inspect it without a warrant?"

"The outside of it, yes, since it's in public view. All the same, it might be best for you to claim the victory if we find anything."

He parked and they both exited and quietly walked to the car parked in the driveway. Penelope didn't know anything about cars, she didn't even yet know how to drive. However, this one looked appropriately sporting for a young man, painted in a cream color with shiny, black leather seats in front and back. Like many cars, it was a convertible, with the top pulled back.

With unspoken agreement, Richard rightly focused on the less legally problematic area of the outside of the car, while Pen stuck her head into the interior. She wasn't quite sure what she was looking for, perhaps a handkerchief with the letters MC embroidered on it?

"Ah-ha," she heard Richard say. Penelope pulled herself back out and swiveled to look down at him where he was literally lying on the ground to inspect the area under the front of the car. She certainly admired his dedication to his job, considering he was ruining his tuxedo. Pen wondered how much it had cost him. She wasn't sure what a detective's salary was, but she imagined it certainly wasn't enough to go through tuxedos like handkerchiefs. Then again, she didn't know much about his financial circumstances. She had only just recently learned about his family.

"What did you find?" Pen came over to hunch down next to him. She wasn't quite as prepared to lie on the ground.

He pulled himself away and came to a seated position, one arm resting on a leg bent up. "Blood."

Pen felt her heart quicken. "This is it, evidence!"

"Good enough. Keep in mind, it could just as easily have been left from hitting a squirrel or pigeon, but this is probably enough for a warrant."

"Humph," Pen groused, racing back to the side of the car. "It's a shame the police didn't have reason to question the Carltons right after it happened. There was probably far more evidence before that bit of rain we had. They could have found Martha's killer before the party. Who knows, maybe James would still be alive because of it! As it is, I plan on rectifying that gross oversight."

"What are you doing?"

"As you stated, I'm not a police officer, I can snoop." With that, she swung open the door and crawled into the car. She contorted herself so she could inspect every nook and cranny, particularly places where the murderer might not have thought to check.

"Yes!" Pen exclaimed when she found a small pink speck hidden in the slight hollow. "Another jellybean, also pink!"

She pulled up with a triumphant look. "Certainly this is enough to question her?"

Richard rose and stuck his head into the car, twisting it awkwardly enough to espy the piece of candy. "This definitely creates a connection."

"What the hell do you think you're doing here?"

That booming voice caught the attention of both Detective Prescott and Penelope. They turned to find Bruce storming out of the front door of the house. Richard stopped him before he could reach the car.

"Mr. Carlton, I'm afraid this vehicle is now evidence in the murder of Martha Combs."

"What the hell do you mean evidence? I wasn't anywhere near Glen Cove that night. In fact—" He instantly shut up, no doubt wisely realizing that anything he said might be used against him.

"So you weren't driving this car three nights ago?"

Bruce's face went perfectly white at that announcement. Of course, most people would be aghast to find their car may have been used as a murder weapon, and she knew she was biased, so she didn't want to jump to conclusions. Still, she hoped that his reaction was due to guilt. She hated to think that Savannah was somehow responsible for Martha's death.

"I'm not saying another word."

"As is your right. However, you are not allowed to so much as touch this car, let alone drive it, do you understand?"

"No, I do not!" Bruce protested. "This is *my* property. You can't just forbid me from using it. How am I to get around?"

"Your property, and yours alone? Not the family's?"

Richard asked. "Would anyone else have had access to it three nights ago?"

Bruce went pale again. "I—well, yes, *anyone* could have used it. In fact, almost everyone staying here has at some point. I'd like to know why you think it's evidence."

"We found blood, among other things."

"Blood?" Bruce repeated. He looked positively bewildered. Either he was shocked at this revelation or just shocked that he'd missed erasing any evidence of his crime. At this point, Penelope wasn't sure who was to blame for Martha's death.

"I'll need to call the Glen Cove police department, since this case is their jurisdiction. May I use your phone?"

Bruce looked ready to protest, then thought better of it. There was no benefit to being difficult at this point. He recomposed himself and angrily gestured toward the door. Richard turned to Penelope to make sure she stayed behind to keep Bruce from approaching the car, then went inside.

"I suppose you're getting no small satisfaction from all of this," Bruce said glaring at her.

"No, I most certainly am not," she retorted. "A woman was murdered. I'd think that would have some effect on you, considering."

"Considering what?"

"Considering you were in a relationship with her."

"How the hell do you know that?" Bruce blurted out. He went pale again when he realized his mistake.

It was too late, and yes, Penelope finally had a small degree of satisfaction. Bruce Carlton had just given himself a motive for murder.

CHAPTER TWENTY

"I'm not saying a word without my attorney present," Bruce insisted, yet again. This time, he wisely kept his mouth shut after that announcement.

Richard had made the call to the Glen Cove police, who were on their way. He came back out to join Bruce and Penelope. Finn followed behind him, a curious look on his face.

"I heard the commotion from my room. What's all this about?" Finn asked.

"We strongly suspect this car was used in the murder of Martha Combs," Richard replied.

"They think it was *your* car?" Finn blurted out, staring at Bruce in shock.

"I didn't murder her, you damn fool!"

Finn swallowed and quickly recomposed himself realizing Richard and Penelope had both turned their attention to him. He met them with a cool, defiant look.

"If it wasn't either of you, then you have nothing to worry about. Answer a few questions and we'll be gone,"

Penelope said. Richard wisely remained silent, considering his jurisdictional murkiness.

"Nice try," Bruce snapped, giving her a venomous look. "I know how that mind of yours works, trapping people with the things they've said or done. You already despise me. You're probably just waiting to trap me with something."

"I can promise you that a few worms down my back have no bearing whatsoever on my prejudice in this case," she said in an airy tone.

"So you say. You've never forgiven me for that, a harmless schoolboy prank. As it is, I would like both of you to leave. You can come back with your warrant and talk to me through my attorney."

"Very well," Pen said making sure to show indifference. "I suppose Morris has retreated to his own home?"

"He'll have nothing to say to you either," Bruce scoffed. "His parents came back yesterday morning. Some hullaballoo over at their place with what Martha did. Besides, he wasn't even here that night, remember? Has that mind of yours gone to rot already, Pen?"

"That's fine, we don't need to talk to him," Pen said, trying a different avenue to get him to blurt out something useful. "After all, Savannah is staying with me. I'm sure she will have something to offer, specifically concerning your whereabouts that night?"

Bruce suddenly looked scared again. "You will not speak to her without an attorney either."

"I'm with Bruce on this. As her brother, her *older* brother, and the one responsible for her welfare, I insist that you wait until an attorney can be brought to counsel her before you begin any interrogations," Finn said, looking almost as worried as Bruce. Pen wondered what it was they were both hiding. "All this over some maid who gets herself run over on some isolated stretch of road in the middle of nowhere. In *your* part of Long Island, I might add! I see no reason why Savannah should become entangled in all of this."

"I'm sure she can decide that for herself," Pen said, already turning to leave. She stopped and twisted around to give him one last look. "If she's the alibi for either of you, you might as well tell us now."

"She—well, of course she is!" Bruce said, his voice transitioning from uncertain to far too overly confident. "Why wouldn't she have been here that night?"

"*I* can confirm that Bruce was here all night," Finn said. "Yes, he was a bit drunk, that's probably why he's avoiding your questions. However, I can confirm as much. We were both here."

"I see, and your sister? Was she here all night as well?"

"She most certainly was."

"How do you know? Were you up all night?" Richard asked. "You didn't go to bed at all?"

"I'm...a light sleeper. And, other than Bruce's, my room is the only one that overlooks the front drive. I would have seen or heard the car leave."

"And as far as you know it didn't?" Pen asked.

"No."

"Then how would you explain the blood underneath the front?"

That seemed to catch him up. He obviously hadn't heard that part.

"Well, I..."

"Don't say another word, Finn," Bruce hissed, his face growing red with anger. "They're trying to trap you. That's why I insisted on an attorney. Finn was only trying to protect me—not that I need it. As I said, please leave now. We have nothing more to say to you or the other officers."

Finn still looked troubled, as though realizing he had caused more problems for Bruce—or perhaps his sister?—than he had solved.

A police car arrived with two Glen Cove officers to take control of the situation. Richard explained that they needed to preserve the car as evidence, instructing them that no one should touch it. He also informed them of what evidence they had found, making sure to mention that it was Pen who had first found the jellybean inside the car. Once everything seemed secured, Richard and Penelope left to head back to Glen Cove.

"They're obviously hiding something. They both looked terrified at the news that the car might have been the one used in Martha's murder."

"I noted that as well," Richard said.

"If both their rooms overlook the drive, one or both of them should have heard the car starting up and leaving unless they were asleep at the time," Pen said.

"And unless Mr. Duncan was lying about being a light sleeper," Richard said.

"Perhaps they were in on it together, both of them conspiring to kill her?"

"For what motive?"

"Bruce pretty much confessed to me that he was having an illicit relationship with Martha."

"He won't make the mistake of admitting that again when the police question him."

"I'm sure Savannah knows. She might be willing to offer a statement. Or perhaps Joan—yes, definitely Joan. She'd be happy to tell us as much."

THE GREAT GASTON MURDER

"Or she just enjoys opening Pandora's box. There's something meddlesome about that one."

"I'm meddlesome," Penelope reminded him with a teasing smile.

"For all the right reasons, Pen my dear."

She grinned, then nibbled her lip in thought. "So, getting back to motive. Perhaps Bruce's relationship went wrong somehow? Wrong enough that he wanted Martha dead? It would have been easy enough to rope Finn into doing his bidding. He definitely has some leverage over Savannah's brother."

"I don't know. Finn seemed pretty shocked when we revealed it was Bruce's car that might have hit Martha," Richard said. "And how do you explain the jellybean we found, or at least what was left of it? Perhaps both of them are covering for Savannah?"

Pen shook her head. "Bruce would never be that chivalrous, especially if it meant his own neck on the line as well. Still, you raise an interesting point."

Pen stared out the window as he turned onto Brookline Drive, passing by the gated homes and long driveways. This had been the same ride Martha had taken the last night of her life. Driven out here by her killer until they were finally alone with nothing but the wilderness to witness—

"Stop the car!"

Once again, Richard came to a screeching halt. "Pen dear," he drawled in a dry tone, "You really are an expert at giving a man a near heart attack."

Penelope was too caught up in the revelation that had just hit her to respond in an equally teasing manner. She turned to Richard with wide eyes.

"I think I know who killed Martha!"

CHAPTER TWENTY-ONE

"We have to do this just right. We can't let either Finn or Bruce know we may have figured it out. More importantly, we have to reassure them that we don't think it's either of them. Otherwise, they'll play the lawyer card again and clam right up. We need them to talk, this time in front of witnesses, specifically those two policemen." Penelope was mostly talking to herself as they raced back to Sands Point and the Carlton home.

"All the better that you're taking the reins on this," Richard said. "You not being officially part of law enforcement does have its benefits, after all, Pen dear."

"I love it when you call me dear. I think you should do it more often," Pen said with a grin. She felt imbued with the excitement that always overcame her when she was on the cusp of solving a murder. Perhaps not the most tasteful state of emotion, but at least Martha Combs might forgive her, since they were about to flush out her killer.

"Yes, dear," Richard said with a grin. Pen smiled, realizing that he had the same thrill running through his veins.

They arrived back at the Carlton home. The two

policemen were sitting in their car, keeping an eye on the car they were supposed to be watching. They saw Detective Prescott and Penelope returning and even before they came to a stop, Pen could see the looks of confusion on their faces. They stepped out of their cars just as Richard parked.

"Did you forget something?" One of the officers asked him when he and Pen stepped out of their cars.

"We just need a few more words with the gentlemen inside," Richard said.

The two officers eyed each other. "I guess if Chief Higgins said it was okay?"

"Absolutely," Pen lied. She flashed a dazzling smile as she boldly rang the doorbell.

The butler answered, but she was prepared for this obstacle. "Hello, we're here to speak to both Finn and Bruce, if you could get them. Please be sure to let them know that Detective Prescott and I, Penelope Banks, know they aren't the ones who killed Martha Combs, but we need to speak to them to clarify a few points and we won't have to ask them any more questions after that."

"Yes, miss," he said, true to his station, he showed no hint of curiosity or fascination. Pen just hoped he worded it correctly when he went to speak to them.

They waited outside on the front steps for what seemed like an eon. Just when Pen began to wonder if she should have used more coercive language, Bruce and Finn came to the front door, both sporting wary expressions.

"Is it true? Have you found the murderer? The *real* murderer?" Bruce asked, scrutinizing them. His gaze flashed to the two policemen who had drawn in closer at the mention of murder.

"We think we have," Penelope said.

"Then what do you need us for?" Finn asked with a frown.

"Perhaps we should still wait for our attorneys, Finn," Bruce warned.

"If you'd like to do that," Richard interjected. "We're only back to clarify a single point about the Martha Combs murder. That, of course, doesn't preclude us from investigating the murder of James Gaston. While we wait for your attorneys to arrive that should give us plenty of time to get a warrant to search the house for anything related to that crime...or others."

"Fine, fine," Bruce snapped, a flash of panic coming to his face. His eyes darted to the policemen standing behind Richard and Penelope. "You might as well come into the sitting room—just the two of you."

That wouldn't work for what Pen had in mind. They needed the policemen to hear the responses, so she spoke quickly. "Oh no, we only need to ask one quick question simply for clarification purposes, then we'll be on our way."

He sighed heavily, just to let them know what an inconvenience this all was. "Fine then, what is it?"

"Earlier when we were talking about Martha's murder, Finn, you mentioned that it could have been anyone who killed her?"

Finn's brow furrowed, wondering if there was some hidden trap in the question. His response was slow and measured. "Yes?"

"Because as you said, she was run over on some isolated stretch of road in the middle of nowhere?"

"Yes," he said, quicker this time but still with a look of caution on his face.

"Perfect, that's all we needed clarification on," she said in a cheery voice.

"That's it?" Bruce asked in surprise.

"Oh yes," Pen said brightly, turning as though to leave. Even the police officers seemed to be mentally scratching their heads. She stopped and turned back. "Actually, there is one more thing."

Bruce pursed his lips as though he knew Richard and she had been lying about this being a quick matter. When he saw her gaze trained on Finn, he followed it.

"How did you know she was killed on an isolated stretch of road in the middle of nowhere, Finn?"

He rapidly blinked. "Well...you told us. That day you came to visit. You told us all about the murder, that it was right there in Glenn Cove on Brookline Drive."

"Yes, but I never said which part of Brookline Drive. So, how did you know it was on the isolated stretch of that road?"

"Well, I—someone else must have told me!"

"Who? You weren't questioned by the police, so it couldn't have been them. I never gave Savannah and Joan any more information than I gave you. At the time, even I didn't know which part of Brookline Drive it had happened on. So who told you?"

"I don't know," he spat, then his eyes widened as a possible explanation came to him. "I must have overheard it at the party."

"That's odd because the only people who would have known were perhaps those questioned by the police. Then again, they never told me which part of Brookline Drive the murder occurred on when I was questioned. I only happened upon it myself, the unfortunate remnant of the murder staining the road."

"That's it!" Finn blurted, his panic overcoming him. "I saw the same evidence on the way to your place."

"For the party?"

"Er, yes," he said hesitantly.

"It couldn't have been because it rained heavily the night after the murder, erasing any evidence away."

"Finn, you bastard!" Bruce exclaimed before Finn could come up with another excuse. "You killed her! And this whole time you made me think it might have been me?" He took hold of Finn's shirt and slammed him against the door.

Pen gasped in surprise. Richard and the officers were quick to step in and pull the two apart. Finn looked perfectly shaken. Bruce was irate, still kicking out and swinging his fists toward him.

"He did it! I'll tell you everything. I came home that night with Martha after spending time in the city. I was so out of it, drunk on bootleg moonshine, I don't even remember what happened after that. Martha was gone and when Finn woke me, he suggested something bad had happened, that he'd cover for me. I didn't even know what until you came that day, Pen. All I did was drive her here to Long Island, I remember that much."

"Yes, you brought that conniving little wench here!" Finn spat. "Everything would have been perfect if not for you! She ruined everything! Snooping where she shouldn't have. And oh did she love rubbing people's faces in the things she found."

"Rubbing your face in what?" Bruce asked, calming down and narrowing his eyes with suspicion. "Are *you* the one who keeps stealing my cufflinks? Was that it? *That's* why you killed her? Because you were worried I'd find out? And all while I agreed to marry that dumb wet blanket of a sister of yours? You thought I would have ended the wedding, didn't you? Well, you would have been right!"

"As though you aren't getting something out of it! If I

have to hear you whine about your trust one more time—it was enough to drive me mad. At least you were getting something from your folks. And you're a fine one to talk about cheating. Bringing that damn maid here, flaunting her around? Letting her wander as though she owned the place? That little tart of yours tried blackmailing me after finding those damn cuff links. Ha! Why the hell did she think I was stealing in the first place? That dumb sap of a husband of hers should be glad I did him the favor of running her over." Finn seemed to sag with the weight of what he'd done. He shook his head with dismay. "If she'd just stayed in the car, and then not tried to run away, it wouldn't have been so... messy. Frankly, I was surprised she originally bought the idea that I needed to drive her someplace to get the money she asked for. But she figured out what I was up to before we got there. I thought it was safe, at least being in an isolated place with no one around."

That explained why there was such a distance from where the jellybean had been found in the grass and where she'd finally been run down.

"So you *did* plan on framing James? That's why you were on your way to Glen Cove with Martha. You planned on killing her there, didn't you? How did you even know about Savannah and James—wait, it was Bruce's telescope, wasn't it? You saw the two of them."

"They weren't exactly discreet! Sitting there right on his porch while that carnival trash painted my sister, as though the world wasn't watching. And Savannah knew how much this idiot liked looking through his telescope like some reprobate," he said, waving a hand at Bruce. "How the hell he missed it, is beyond me. Then again, he was probably focused on more prurient things."

"Shut up!" Bruce said.

THE GREAT GASTON MURDER

Finn just laughed bitterly. "And who could blame her for going behind your back? At least James respected her. If it wasn't for the money I never would have agreed to this pathetic marriage."

"Well, enjoy it from prison!" Bruce spat.

Finn just glowered back at him.

That seemed to be the end of it. With as much of a confession as they were going to get, and it was certainly a doozy, the police officers were happy to arrest Finn for the murder of Martha Combs.

"Did you kill James too?" Penelope asked.

"Of course he killed James!" Bruce protested. "Isn't it obvious? That would explain everything!"

Finn gave Pen a confused look as the handcuffs were placed on him. "Why would I bother? Savannah assured me she had no intention of leaving Bruce for James. I don't even have a gun."

"But then how—" Bruce seemed confused, then realized that if Finn had no reason to kill James it still left him looking like the guilty party. He once again shut up.

"With Savannah's reassurances she was going to marry Bruce, I had no reason to kill James. I just needed the money to pay off my debts. That's all I ever cared about."

"That and not getting caught having stolen from me!" Bruce groused.

The police put Finn in the car and called the station to handle finalizing the conclusion to this particular murder.

"There's still the problem of the jellybean," Richard said, pulling Penelope aside. "How did it get on the side of the road?"

"Savannah mentioned something about Bruce searching through her things. I don't think it was him, I think it was Martha. Both Finn and Morris said something about her having a bad habit of snooping. Savannah had a stash of jellybeans in one of her dresser drawers. Martha must have helped herself to some while she was exploring. I suppose that's also how she discovered Finn was stealing from Bruce. She must have found the stolen cufflinks." She smiled, though it was tepid. "And all this time Bruce thought it was Joan."

"Well, that's one murder down. We still need to figure out who killed James."

"Yes," Penelope said with a sigh. "First, we should go back and at least give Savannah the news about her brother. She might also be able to shed some more light on who might have wanted James dead."

CHAPTER TWENTY-TWO

Back at the house, Chief Higgins was blessedly somewhere else, and thus unable to intervene with questions or comments about what had just taken place at the Carlton home. It would take time for the news about Finn to trickle back to him while he was here. In the meantime, several policemen still lingered about the property.

Before they searched for Savannah, Penelope allowed Richard the dignity of at least quickly changing into something more appropriate than his ruined tuxedo. When he came back, they were drawn to the parlor where Joan was entertaining Benny, Lulu, Jane, and Alfie with some story. They had all changed out of their glad rags and were helping themselves to what was left in the bottles from the party, of which there were far too many. Cousin Cordelia was hopefully in a blissful state of brandy-induced sleep upstairs.

Savannah was off somewhere else, it seemed.

"One would have never known a murder had just taken place," Penelope said, giving them all a scolding look.

"All the more reason to enjoy life's pleasures, darling. One never knows when their time is up. As James has so definitively shown us," Joan said, lifting her glass towards Pen.

"How is the investigation going?" Lulu asked. She was infused with her usual insouciance, but Pen could see the worry in her dark eyes. They still had James's murder to solve, which was the one that she would most likely be caught up in, since her prints were likely on the gun. Of course, Pen would never have allowed that to happen, but she could understand her concern.

"We're getting closer." It wasn't much, but Pen offered what she hoped was a reassuring smile before continuing. "Where is Savannah? We need to speak with her for a moment." Pen didn't want to reveal that the police had arrested Finn before telling his sister first.

"She's being perfectly morose on the steps outside. I suggest you hurry, the poor dear may very well throw herself in the sea and turn to foam just like the little mermaid when she lost her love!" Joan said, dramatically waving toward the windows that faced the sound.

Her cavalier attitude was beginning to wear on Pen. Yes, in her experience, people had wildly different reactions to death, and more so murder. But this was a bit much.

The others hid their mix of embarrassment and disapproval behind their drinks. Even Benny cast a censuring eye on Joan, and he was usually the most inappropriate member of their group.

Richard and Pen departed, going through the foyer toward the French doors that led outside. They found Savannah sitting on the top step at the edge of the terrace, still in her party dress as she stared out at the water. Her hair was now loose, falling down her back in waves that did almost make her look like Ariel from the fairy tale. Though she must have heard them, she only acknowledged them when they descended to the steps just below her and forced her attention away from the water.

"Did you learn anything?" She asked, looking only mildly curious, as though it didn't really matter to her either way.

Pen decided to be the one to break the news to her. "The police have arrested your brother for the murder of Martha Combs."

That was enough to spark her interest. "Finn? Why would he have killed her?"

"It seemed she may have been the one who was going through your things back at the house. She also discovered that Finn was stealing from Bruce, the cufflinks?"

Savannah exhaled, as though that answered some question for her. A cynical smile hitched one side of her mouth. "He couldn't help himself. Even now, after everything that I agreed to, he's still gambling, I suppose."

Penelope and Richard briefly eyed one another.

"Gambling?" Richard pressed.

"Finn has massive debts, enough that our parents have cut him off. Lately, he's racked up enough that...well, I thought it was only right that I help him. These people he owes aren't exactly the type to collect via the courts."

"That's why you agreed to marry Bruce," Pen confirmed, unable to hide the pity in her voice. There were times she rued never having had a sibling growing up. Moments like this made her rethink that. "I don't mean to offend but, why Bruce? Just because he and Finn were friends? Surely there were other wealthy young men you could marry?"

Savannah's gaze sharpened. Something in the way she

now stared back at both of them made Pen think about what Joan had said about her having a bit of mettle in her. "It wasn't just for Finn's sake. In fact, that was simply an added benefit. But I suppose that is moot now if he's going to prison."

"What do you mean it wasn't just for Finn's sake?"

Savannah took a breath as she focused on Penelope in particular. Something flitted across her eyes, a flash of guilt or regret before they steeled again.

"James and I had a plan. Not just to run off together, but to have money when we did. It would solve all our problems and allow us to have what we most wanted—each other."

"Now, I'm the one who doesn't quite understand," Richard said.

Savannah kept her eyes on Penelope, waiting to see if she would figure it out. It took a moment, but then everything fell into place.

"*That's* why you showed no indication you were leaving Bruce. You never intended to cancel the wedding and run away with James. You wanted to marry Bruce and then divorce him on the grounds of infidelity, walking away with a nice tidy sum of his money."

A slow smile spread Savannah's lips. For the first time, she looked like something other than the meek little lamb she'd been portraying all this time. If anything, she resembled a she-wolf at the moment.

"He's had trysts, affairs, flings, and relationships of every kind, with every kind of woman the entire time we've been together. He flaunts it. I knew nothing would change once we were married, including his inability to keep from making his affairs public. I could stomach a few years of marriage to him if it meant ending it all and being with

James without having to worry about money, either for my brother or the two of us. We could go back to Paris and live as artists without worry."

"But why bring James into it at all? Him coming back? Wouldn't his presence just hamper those plans?"

The note of cynicism came back to Savannah's face. "Not at all. Once, in a moment of weakness—I was just so fed up with Bruce's horrible behavior—I threatened to end our relationship. I told him there was someone else, someone I loved and would rather be with." She exhaled a sharp laugh. "He was in a rage over that. I thought he might become violent with jealousy, and end it all. But I learned that jealousy was the one way to cement our engagement more than anything else. He proposed the next day and told me that no one was taking me from him—no one.

"James coming back was meant to hurry the marriage along. Get him to finally set a date. We didn't want to make it too obvious, of course. Still, after so long apart...we couldn't help sneaking around to see one another. It wouldn't do for him to have caught us in the act. Thus, I only came to visit him by boat after I assumed everyone was asleep—or when Bruce was out with one of his little girlfriends."

"What would Bruce have done if he had caught you and James together in a...compromising way?" Pen asked.

Savannah met her with a level gaze. "With the amount of pride he has? I have no doubt he would have killed him."

"He did know about my gun after all," Pen agreed.

"He was also more than willing to give his fingerprints" Richard reminded her.

"He also has his own gun collection," Savannah said. "I assume the police will be looking there at some point?"

"Based on Finn's confession, we might be able to get a

warrant for his room, but I imagine the Carltons will put up a strong front to fight us searching any other areas of the house."

"Bruce had been rather skittish about the police searching his home," Penelope noted.

"Most people are," Richard countered.

She thought back over the past several days, wondering if something would jump out at her as it had in the case of Finn and Martha. Nothing came to her, at least not yet. But one thing certainly did, something that Savannah might just be able to clarify.

"Tell me what you know about Lawrence Whittaker."

Savannah didn't seem surprised by the name, though there was a brief flicker of something fierce and alarming that flashed in her eyes.

"I wondered when you might bring him up."

"So you know him? Was he really James's representative for his art?"

Savannah coughed out a sharp laugh. She tilted her head and considered Penelope. "James was worried about you figuring it out, at least earlier than he wanted."

"I take it that's a no," Pen replied in an impatient voice.

"No, he isn't. Lawrence Whittaker is...James's grandfather."

Penelope stood up straighter in surprise, reconfiguring everything in her memory so that it now made complete sense. "Yes, they have the same eyes; except an aquamarine shade rather than green."

Savannah nodded, a sad smile coming to her face as she no doubt recalled James's most attractive feature.

"And he thought James owed him something? Why? Just for leaving the carnival?"

"Lawrence is like that," she said with a frown. "He likes

THE GREAT GASTON MURDER

to use people. Feels that any slight benefit he's done for anyone, they owe him back ten times over. He is good at either charming or intimidating people into getting his way, or just using blackmail. He is also quite cunning. He liked to belittle James for contributing nothing to the carnival growing up. Felt he needed to make up for it somehow as an adult. That's why Agnes sent him to Paris so quickly. She didn't want Lawrence to learn about it, so it was hushed up. Of course, he eventually found out. Only when he realized James was practically a starving artist over there did he relent. At least until Agnes died. He thought maybe James would inherit something, and he could profit somehow."

"Why didn't James just say no? Surely, he wasn't that intimidated by a man he hadn't even seen in almost five years?"

Savannah's expression changed, taking on a slightly sheepish look. "James and I never stopped writing to one another. Even when I became engaged, we were in constant contact...making plans. He must have known what we were up to, probably threatened to tell Bruce."

"I see." Penelope didn't fault them. Considering what a scoundrel Bruce was, he deserved this. After all, he was using Savannah just as much as she had been using him.

Still, one thing nagged at her. "Why did Agnes go to all this trouble to help James in the first place? He claimed his mother worked at one of her parties, but I've been told that was unlikely. What is his connection to her?"

Savannah stared at Penelope for a long time before answering. "You are, Penelope. You're the connection."

She blinked in response. Richard took a step closer to her, as though he knew something was coming that might make her reel.

"Your mother and Agnes were quite close, no?"

"Yes," Penelope said, nearly breathless. "What does that have to do with James?"

Now Savannah looked sympathetic. "Lawrence wasn't only James's grandfather. He's yours as well."

CHAPTER TWENTY-THREE

Penelope did in fact reel at the news Savannah had just imparted. Richard was quick to bring a strong arm around her to hold her up when her knees went weak.

"What do you mean Lawrence is my grandfather?"

"Lawrence Whittaker's real name is Leonard Williams. James's real last name is Williams as well," Savannah replied. "He changed it before he moved to Paris. Agnes and his mother didn't want his grandfather to find him, so they helped him with that. It was the name they told to anyone who may have asked about him. James kept the name change, wanting nothing to do with Lawrence once he left. Of course, a man like that eventually finds out."

Penelope's head was filled with far too many questions. How did her mother, born Juliette Williams, end up in a theater in San Francisco if she had been raised in a carnival that traveled along the east coast?

"That's why Agnes was willing to help James," Savannah continued. "His mother, your aunt, came to her—or rather, she came to your mother and pleaded with her to help him escape. Carnival life was slowly destroying him. He was made for greater things. If you see his art, you would understand, especially now that he's finally grown into it. It's his passion, his life."

Right now, Penelope didn't much care about James's art or his passion. Why was she just now learning about all of this? Her mother's past had always been a mystery to Pen. She had died not too long after she'd helped send James to France. Why hadn't she told Pen she had a cousin? An aunt? A grandfather? Why hadn't Agnes?

But they were dead now, their secrets taken with them. The only person left who could give Penelope any information about this man was—

"My father," she said to Richard rather than Savannah. "We need to see him, now!"

Without waiting for an answer she stormed back up the stairs to the back terrace, past the tables and stands, torn streamers and deflated balloons, rapidly decaying food, and back inside. Richard, fully understanding her intent, followed her through the front doors and outside again.

"Miss Banks? Detective Prescott?" Chief Higgins called out in protest, obviously back from wherever he had been. "We need to discuss this business about the Martha Combs—"

"Not now, Chief Higgins," Richard said in that voice of his that instantly got anyone to obey. He led Penelope back to his car and opened the passenger side door for her. He got in on the driver's side and sped them away.

"It's Sunday, he'll be at home," she said, and Richard nodded. Penelope's father lived on 5th Avenue, just as she did, about ten blocks south of her. He'd been to Penelope's apartment building enough for her to have pointed out the mansion she'd grown up in.

Interestingly enough, it had been another murder case in which her father had told Pen that she should let go of the idea of learning anything about her mother's side of the family. It seemed murder and her mother's past went hand in hand.

What had her father been trying to hide all this time?

There was silence for a good five minutes before Penelope finally spoke again. "What I don't understand is that they *all* knew. My mother, Agnes, and even my father. Why would they keep this from me? What was so terrible about James? About Lawrence—Leonard, I suppose his name is?"

"Perhaps it was the other way around? Maybe your mother's family kept their distance for some reason?"

Penelope was silent for a moment, something about what Richard had said triggering a dark thought in her mind. Finally, she responded. "I doubt that. If Lawrence really has as much avarice as Savannah suggested, and even James at one point, then he would have gladly made himself known to me. After all, I've been a millionaire for the past seven months," she said numbly.

Richard didn't speak at first. "Are you certain you don't want to take some time to absorb this before...talking to your father?"

"You mean confronting him? Learning something horrible? No, I don't. I'm done with all the secrecy. Besides, he may know where Leonard is. He could still be James's killer, after all."

Richard simply nodded.

Penelope remained quiet for the rest of the ride in. She thought about the first time Richard had driven her into Manhattan from Long Island. She hadn't thought much of him as a detective at that point. In fact, she'd been rather vexed with his dry humor in response to her questioning his competency. But even then, she'd thought him handsome, even with the same scar that she had a perfect view of right now as she sat next to him in the car.

Richard was an anchor, she realized. Someone she could rely on to be there for her, protect her, secure her in a storm of messiness, and even put her in her place when she needed it. He made her laugh, drove her mad, and stirred a heat in her that he was more than capable of sating quite well. Most of all she felt safe with him.

How would he take to learning whatever he learned about her mother today?

She felt deep inside that he would still be there for her, perhaps more than ever. It was the one reassurance she had with the uncertainty that this case had created—about everyone she had thought she knew.

As they got nearer to Central Park Pen felt her body go tense. Richard went up Madison Avenue and turned onto 62nd to park. She felt a resurgence of indignation and rabid curiosity spur her right out of the car. She flew ahead of him down the sidewalk and to the front door. Richard sped up to be next to her as soon as she rang the bell.

Coleman, the same butler who had worked there when she was a child answered. He briefly noted Richard, with nothing more than a polite blink.

"Miss Penelope," he greeted in his usual familiar way, something she hoped never changed. Though, right now she was in no mood to be nostalgic.

"I have to talk to father," she said, storming in past him before he could even respond.

Pen was certain that behind her Richard was offering Coleman an apologetic smile as he followed her in. She stopped in the foyer, realizing she had no idea which room her father might be in, or even if he was home right now. He wasn't one to "waste perfectly valuable time in church," so she needn't have worried about that.

"Where is he, Coleman?"

"If you'll follow me," he said cordially, as though she hadn't brought a perfect hurricane into the calm serenity of the home. "Your father is presently meeting with someone, but I can announce you, if you'll have a seat in the parlor?"

Being told to wait in the parlor of what used to be her own home rankled her a bit, but her father certainly wouldn't have had it any other way. Who could he even be meeting with on a Sunday?

Pen didn't bother sitting down. She was too filled with energy and impatience to do something so sedate. Richard stood by the window watching her with mild concern on his face. Pen hoped he wouldn't do something as silly as ask if she was okay.

Because she most certainly wasn't.

When Coleman came back she nearly jumped like a startled cat. "Mr. Banks will see you now," he said as though her entire world wasn't erupting around her.

At least he hurried as he led them to the study. Pen still had to keep herself from running to beat him to the door. When he finally opened it, she felt another eruption in her life, this one larger than any of the others.

"You!" Pen said, staring at the man with whom her father was meeting: Leonard Williams.

Now, she saw the family resemblance. Those vivacious green eyes that seemed to perpetually twinkle with some mischief were her mother's eyes in every way—even in color. They were also James's, though his had a tinge of blue to camouflage the resemblance.

Coleman left, wisely closing the door behind him.

"Miss Banks, so lovely to see you again!" Leonard said with a beaming smile. "I was visiting your father for a little, ah, renegotiation. I thought it appropriate considering the circumstances."

"Is that what kept you away from me all these years?" Pen wasn't sure on whom to cast her look of resentment, her father or her grandfather.

"I see you've met your grandfather, Penelope," her father said, his voice filled with controlled anger.

Penelope shifted her outrage to her father. "Yes, I have, with no assistance from you, I might add."

"And there's a very good reason for that," her father retorted, casting a stony look at Leonard.

Pen's grandfather—the idea was still quite alien to her—looked on with cheerful indifference. "How fortuitous, a family reunion. I see we even have a handsome suitor to join in?" He said, giving Richard a questioning look.

"Perhaps it's best if we had this meeting alone, Penelope," Her father said.

"No," Pen said, she gave Leonard a hard look."*Detective* Prescott is here with me in an official capacity. It *is* rather fortuitous, this little family reunion, though I could hardly call it a reunion, considering I've never been properly introduced to you. I came here to ask my father where I might be able to locate you. It seems you've saved me the trouble. We need to question you about the murder of your grandson, Mr. Whittaker. Or should I call you Leonard Williams?"

"Murder?" Reginald exclaimed. He turned to Leonard. "What have you done now, Leonard?"

"Now, why would I murder my own grandson, Miss Banks? Can I call you, Penelope? Seeing as how we've officially become acquainted?"

"No."

He laughed softly, which made Pen's ire grow. "Perhaps once we get to know one another, you'll change your mind."

"That's not going to happen," her father said in a dark voice.

"I think I can speak for myself, father. Particularly since you seem to have spoken for me in this matter all of my life."

"And for very good reason," he said, turning to her. "If you want to blame someone, it was at your mother's insistence. Though it was an idea with which I wholeheartedly agreed. Nothing good will come from getting to know this man, Penelope."

"That's a bit harsh, don't you think, Reginald?" Leonard said with a mocking expression of hurt on his face.

"You did enough damage as it is, I won't have you corrupting my daughter in the same manner."

"Corrupting me how?" Penelope said, practically yelling.

"I think perhaps I should, in fact, leave," Richard said quietly.

"No," Pen said. She reached out and took his hand, physically keeping him there. She squeezed perhaps a bit too tightly, but it had him squeezing back in reassurance. She glared at Leonard. "Besides, it might be useful to our *murder* case."

Her father sat back in his chair, considering Leonard. "I think I'll let you tell her, Leonard. I, for one, would like to see what balderdash you manage to spin, perverting it into something palatable."

Leonard sported a self-effacing smile as he focused on Penelope. "There really isn't anything all that scandalous involved. Your mother was a very beautiful, very talented young lady, too good to be wasted in the carnival. A diamond in a sea of lowly pebbles. I realized that early on, as did everyone else. A producer visiting the show noted just how lovely and gifted she was. I, being the indulgent father that I am, allowed her to spread her wings on the stage in San Francisco by giving her permission to join his company."

"Sold her to him, you mean. For the pathetic sum of five hundred dollars. All when she was only sixteen, too young to fend for herself or realize what she had been sold into."

"What?" Penelope asked, realizing she was squeezing Richard's hand hard enough to hurt him. He didn't make a sound, but he did step closer to her.

"You make it sound so debauched, Reginald. He was a legitimate producer for a legitimate theater. He made your mother a star."

"As Sylvine Jade," Pen said, revealing the name that had been divulged to her during that earlier case.

"So you've heard of her?" Leonard said, looking pleasantly surprised. He turned to Reginald with a taunting smirk. "See? A star. Who knows what she would have become had you not absconded with her? Perhaps a star on the silver screen?"

"Don't try to paint it as something rosy. Penelope should know how manipulated and exploited her mother was. Worked to the point of exhaustion and madness, all for little to no pay. Bound to a contract that the devil himself would have balked at."

"Yes, it was fortunate she had you to play the white knight, coming in to rescue her." Leonard's eyes took on a taunting gleam. "Or should I say, bought her? Tsk, tsk, Reginald. You know what they say about pots and kettles…"

Pen shot her father an incredulous look. He sat up straighter with umbrage. "I paid to release her from that

THE GREAT GASTON MURDER

devilish servitude she was bound to. It was the only way to free her. I regret nothing. I was...very much in love with her," he said, choking up slightly.

Now Penelope had to rethink their entire marriage. Juliette had been nineteen when her father married her. Did she love Reginald in the same way he had her? Had she simply married him out of gratitude? Or was it because she had nowhere else to turn?

No, Penelope recalled the way her mother looked at her father, the way the two of them interacted. While there may not have been the unbridled passion Pen often felt when she was with Richard, there was respect, fondness, and a certain kind of love. It was certainly more than she could say for many marriages she had seen, especially those that took place during that period among certain classes.

She hated Leonard all the more for making her wonder in the first place.

"And him," Penelope said, jerking her chin Leonard's way. She couldn't bring herself to utter his name. "Why has he been kept from me this entire time?"

"Yes, Reginald, why?" Leonard repeated, turning to her father with a taunting smile.

"I paid him to stay away. Something else of which I have no regrets. Your mother more than anyone knew how easy it would be for him to charm his way into your good graces. She made me promise as much even as that damnable flu took her from us. I have quite willingly honored her wishes."

"But none of that matters now that we've finally met," Leonard turned to Pen with a sorrowful look. "All those years. To think of the important life events I've missed, playing with you as a child, watching you grow up into a fine young woman, guiding you through life's bumps in the road."

Penelope's jaw nearly fell. "I still don't know if you killed James!"

"Ah yes, that nasty bit of business. Rest assured dear granddaughter, it wasn't me. I'm not in the habit of killing kin."

"Just using them for your own financial gain," her father accused.

Leonard sighed. "I suppose, in order to clear my good name, I must confess that yes, I had hoped to use James in order to find my way into your life. When I lost his mother, it occurred to me that you and he were the only blood I had left."

"You had five years to do it. Why now?" Pen asked, challenging him to admit the truth. That it was only when Agnes died and left almost everything to Pen that he had any interest in being a part of her life.

"I can see you suspect the worst of me," he said with a deep frown. "In which case, let me ask you: why would I have killed him?"

"Because he refused to help you try and swindle me, maybe he even threatened to tell me what you were up to."

"But then he would have had to confess himself. James was just as mercenary as I was, my dear Penelope."

"I already know about his plan with Savannah. She told me. I even heard you two fighting about it that day you came to Long Island."

His brow furrowed in confusion, then a smile crept to his face. "It wasn't that silly girl we were fighting about, it was you. His original plan was to use you, my dear. All to keep his precious beloved from marrying that horrid man."

Pen thought back to that argument she'd heard: *You're*

here now with her? *Suddenly, you want to throw it all away?* She had thought they'd been talking about Savannah, but it seemed Leonard had been referring to her. She also remembered what James had said to her later on, when she thought he had also been talking about Savannah: *I'm doing what's best for both of us, Penelope. Trust me.*

Pen shook her head. "No, he wasn't going to use me. He'd made it quite apparent many times, I just didn't have all the pieces to fit it together properly. You'll have to do better than that to clear your name. As far as I'm concerned, you're still a suspect in James's murder."

Leonard sighed heavily yet again. "I had hoped to avoid this, being the gentleman that I am. However, at the time the screaming started, when James was killed I was, *ahem*, entertaining the affections of Miss Windfall, the—" He grimaced with distaste. "—rather *tenacious* woman you were with the day I met you. You can ask her if you must. It's only fair that I tell you I relieved her of some of her baubles. I felt I was owed, as her company was rather exhausting."

"We are going to get in touch with her to make sure."

He simply smiled, unconcerned. Either he would make a very good poker player—and Penelope wouldn't have been at all surprised if he was—or he was telling the truth.

"When you do confirm, I hope we can start off with a clean slate of sorts. I realize today has not left you with the most glowing impression of me. I would hope to rectify that," he said with an overtly endearing look.

"Surely you aren't serious? You sold my mother into... God knows what. You were more than happy to be paid off to avoid me my entire life. Now, conveniently enough when I'm a millionaire, you want to get to know me? I think not!"

He studied her, his shrewdness suddenly coming to the

surface. "How about your mother? Surely you're curious to know more about her? What she was like as a precocious child—perhaps not so unlike yourself? The slight rivalry between her and James's mother, Lorraine? Her first loves? Fears? Dreams? The things every young woman would like to know about her own dearly departed mother? I can tell you everything, Penelope."

Despite herself, Pen felt the fierce tug of curiosity and longing. What had her mother been like as a child? Did he have photographs? Would she have also been the sort of girl to smear mud into a boy's face as an act of revenge? Her mother almost never talked about the period before she met Pen's father, including her childhood. It was a reminder of who she was dealing with.

"For a price, I assume," Penelope scoffed.

He smiled and shrugged, as though that much were obvious.

She stared at him, suddenly realizing why her parents had kept him out of her life. As tempting as his offer was—Penelope had always lived with a fascination of her mother, who had come from nothing and risen to become the darling of the money set in Manhattan—she wasn't willing to go that far to accept it.

"I know all I need to know about my mother. I'd rather hold onto those memories. I also know why James's mother, my aunt, wanted to get him as far as possible away from you. I hope you're happy with the lot you've made for yourself in life because it's all you'll have. I want nothing to do with you."

For the first time, his expression didn't look so cheerful. "You're going to regret this one day. When I'm gone, so too will all my secrets and memories about your family."

Pen ignored him in favor of her father. Something

unspoken passed between them. It was one more step toward the reconciliation that had thawed the ice between them over the past several months. Richard squeezed her hand, reminding her that he was right by her side as well.

"I have the only family I need in my life. One that will never include you."

CHAPTER TWENTY-FOUR

Penelope had left Leonard and her father to finalize the details of their "renegotiation," or rather the "termination." Now that Penelope was fully aware of who her grandfather was and why he had been paid to stay away, there was no need for such an understanding between the two men.

Although she would have liked to properly introduce Richard, she realized it wasn't the time. Perhaps it was best that way. This was the second time her father had seen Richard stand by her side when she needed him most. Surely it had left a good first impression for when they finally did have a formal meeting.

For now, they still had James's murder to solve.

Richard had used a phone in her father's study to place a call to Gilda Windfall. After expressing her outrage that Richard would suggest something so unseemly of her as "behaving unseemly with a perfect miscreant," she had gone into a tirade about her missing silver bracelets. She had been decidedly colorful in her language regarding "Mr. Whittaker," but had eventually confirmed that yes, she had been with him once the screaming started. Which confirmed her grandfather wasn't James's killer.

They had bought two boxes of Cracker Jacks and two bottles of Coca-Cola, as neither of them had eaten anything since the party had been so rudely interrupted by murder. They were enjoying both on the car ride back to Long Island.

"Well, now you've learned even more about my family. Are you sure you still want to hitch your wagon to this ride?" Penelope said, trying to sound lighthearted, but even she could hear the bitterness and unease in her voice.

Richard just smiled as he stared ahead at the road. "You have yet to meet mine. You may just find *your* horse galloping away as quickly as possible.'"

It was enough to make Penelope laugh, and she relaxed into her seat. She stared out the window at the passing scenery.

"I suppose I understand why everyone kept James away. It was probably for his own good as much as mine. He would have been so manipulated by that man." She still couldn't utter his name without contempt. "I still hate that I only had a few days with him before he was killed. Now, more than ever I want to find out who did this."

"If it wasn't your grandf—Mr. Williams, that leaves only a handful of suspects."

"I'm one hundred percent certain it's Bruce, it has to be. Though I suppose Darren is still a likely suspect. Joan and Morris at least knew of him and, more importantly, also knew about my gun, but I can't think of a motive for either of them."

"Let's just make sure it was your gun used."

"Yes, of course," Pen agreed, though she couldn't imagine why or how it wouldn't be. "In the meantime, I suppose we're back to doing good old-fashioned detective work."

Richard briefly turned to her with a grin. "You mean no relying on your womanly wiles?"

"I wouldn't go that far," she said in a saucy tone making them both laugh. After a moment she said, "thank you for that, back in my father's study?"

He turned back to her with a considering look, the same one he'd sported when he first laid eyes upon her, as though he was looking just beyond the surface to read something deeper.

"Of course, Pen dear." Penelope breathed out a small laugh. It led to perfect elation when he reached out to take her hand.

When they arrived back at the mansion, there seemed to be a distinct buzz in the air. The police were still around, but they looked excitedly agitated.

"There must be a development in the case," Richard said as he parked. He and Penelope hurriedly exited the car and ascended the stairs to the front door.

Chives was quick to greet them. "Chief Higgins is here, Miss Banks. He would like to speak with both of you. He's in the parlor with Miss Simmons and Miss Dyson."

Penelope eyed Richard, feeling her worry set in. They had definitely checked the fingerprints against the gun and the box and found only three matching sets, Joan's, Lulu's, and Pen's.

When they reached the parlor, the chief had a look on his face like that of the cat who ate the canary. Joan was sporting her usual look of amused indifference. Lulu put on a good facade, but Pen could tell when she was nervous, and right now it was quite obvious.

"Miss Banks, so happy you could finally join us," Chief

Higgins said smugly. "Now we have all three likely candidates who may have fired your gun." He made sure to add in a dry tone, "*If* it was in fact used in the murder, of course."

"I take it you've finished matching the fingerprints," Pen said.

"We have. As you might imagine this case is a priority. We found only three sets of prints that matched. And yes, all three were on almost every inch of that gun and over every part of that box, top, sides, and bottom: Miss Dyson's, Lucille's, and yours, Miss Banks."

She noted how he didn't use a formal address for her friend, which gave her a bad feeling.

"Well, of course they would be found on every inch. I told your man as much. Even Richard can testify that all three of us touched the box and the gun."

"One moment," Richard interjected. "Did you say the top, sides, and bottom? As in the bottom of the box, not just the sides near the bottom?"

"Yes, the entire thing."

"So fingerprints from all three women matched those found on the very bottom of the box?"

"Yes, the *very bottom of the box*," the chief replied in an overly patient tone, as though he was speaking to an idiot.

Richard turned to Penelope with one eyebrow quirked. She stared back, wondering what he was hinting at. For once, she was the clueless one who had no idea what he was—

"Joan!" Pen swiveled her head to stare at her. "You never touched the bottom of the box that night I received the gun!"

Joan breathed out a humorless laugh and slowly clapped twice. "And thus the mouse is trapped."

"Are you confessing to the murder of James Gaston,

Miss Dyson?" Chief Higgins asked, unable to mask his dumbfounded surprise.

"Of course not," she said with another laugh. "What possible reason would I have to kill him?"

"What possible reason would you have to break into the room and take the box and gun in the first place?" Richard countered.

"And then fire it," Pen added.

"I assure you, it wasn't the gun used in his murder. In fact, I can show you the exact tree trunk I fired it into, conveniently enough while the fireworks were still going—very much *after* poor James was killed."

"But why?" Penelope was the first to ask.

Joan simply gave her a pert look, not answering. Which was smart.

"Miss Dyson?" Chief Higgins prodded in a harsh tone. "I suggest you answer the questions being posed to you. You're in a nice pile of trouble as it is."

"She won't answer," Pen said, eyeing Joan. "She doesn't have to. But it's obvious that she wanted to frame someone, isn't that so, Joan?"

The only indication Joan gave that Pen was right was a slight narrowing of the eyes.

"Who?" Richard asked, studying her to see if he could figure it out.

"Either Savannah, Finn, or Bruce," Pen mused, trying to work it out in her head. "I think it was the former. Earlier in the library, you made it seem as though you hadn't told Bruce and his friends about the gun. If not for Savannah speaking up to contradict that, the focus would have been limited to only those at the dinner that night, including you and Savannah. You were trying to frame Savannah."

Joan exhaled with exasperation and rolled her eyes. "Pen, I'm disappointed in you."

That wasn't the reaction Penelope had been expecting. She stared at Joan waiting for her to reveal what she meant by that. When it was obvious she wasn't going to say anything, Pen thought back to that moment in the library.

"Ahh," she said with sudden understanding. "You didn't want *Bruce* to think you were trying to make *him* look guilty."

"Once again, brava, darling."

"What does all of this have to do with you firing the gun? Did you or did you not set out to frame Mr. Carlton for this murder, Miss Dyson?" Chief Higgins asked in frustration.

"Not at all. One thing you *won't* accuse me of is premeditation," she scoffed. Then, that sly smile came back to her face. "I simply took advantage of an opportunity afforded me. I'm nothing if not quick-thinking."

"Some might call that crafty," Pen said.

"Those people have never had their rightful inheritance snatched from them," Joan snapped, for once showing an emotion other than amusement or indifference. "And for what? I haven't done half the things Bruce has done; haven't embarrassed the family nearly as much. Plus, I'm older by six months! But he's a *man* so he gets away with it. Grandmother always doted on the boys, laughing at their evil little pranks and temper tantrums, as though it were simply a part of their nature. But when I embrace what's in my nature? Wearing pants? Smoking cigarettes? Refusing to marry? I'm ousted from the clan, a black sheep."

"So it boiled down to simple jealousy?" Pen said.

"Oh for heaven's sake, it was obvious Bruce killed James. Who else would it have been? That fellow, Darren, had been sent on his way. Finn is too much of a pantywaist to commit murder—though it seems I was wrong on that count. No one else had a motive. I simply made things more obvious just in case Brucie-boy was by some miracle of miracles smart enough to cover his tracks.

"As I said, the fireworks were still conveniently going off when I first heard the woman scream that someone had been shot. When I heard Savannah scream his name, I figured Bruce had finally taken things a step too far. Pen had carelessly told the *entire world* where her gun was. I knew Agnes's room was at the end of the wing she had added to the house. Everyone was running in the opposite direction. I'm a fast sprinter and I was close enough to it at any rate. I was, quite frankly, surprised when I had the entire area to myself with no one around to see me. So, I broke in."

Joan shrugged as though she had done nothing more than steal a cookie from the cookie jar. In response to the looks of disapproval from the others, she returned an expression of mock regret. "What? It was a good plan, no? Honestly, if I hadn't remembered that I never touched the bottom of the box when I first held the gun, you would have never sniffed me out. However, just in case you're thinking of laying James's murder at my feet, while he was shot, I was chatting with a delightful young gymnast who had stopped in anticipation of the fireworks show. Céline was her name. I'm sure whoever you hired to put this party together—and despite everything, it was simply *fabulous*, Pen darling—they can find her to confirm as much."

"We'll definitely be confirming that," Chief Higgins said in a disgruntled tone.

"Bruce does have his own gun collection, you know. He doesn't miss an opportunity to show them off. You should look into that," Joan said, confirming what they had already been told.

"I don't suppose jealousy is enough probable cause for a warrant?" Penelope asked. Richard shook his head, and she nodded with understanding. "Besides, we still don't have *confirmation* that Bruce even knew about Savannah and James prior to the party."

"Oh for heaven's sake, anyone could see how positively moony Savannah was for James back at the house. They couldn't keep their eyes off one another in that sitting room. Even a dolt like Bruce would have had to notice. So, he makes sure he has his gun on him when he arrives. He knew there would be fireworks, which would have given him the perfect opportunity. Yes, Savannah making such a scene may have thrown the ship off course a bit. Bruce has always been so quick to ignite. Still, he's also always been bitterly vengeful."

Pen could attest to that. Even now she snaked her back a bit, remembering those worms. Still, something Joan had said had sparked something in her head, a loose connection that she knew would make it all make sense...if she could just put her finger on it.

She felt both Richard and Chief Higgins studying her to see if she had any insight or more questions. Pen bit her lip and shook her head in consternation. *Pineapples*, she cursed to herself.

"Miss Dyson, you're going to show me where you fired that gun, then I'm arresting you for burglary," Chief Higgins said.

"Really now, is that necessary?" Joan asked.

"And that's just the first of the charges," he snapped, his frustration getting the better of him. Joan's look of dry amusement disappeared once again when she realized she

THE GREAT GASTON MURDER

was finally getting her comeuppance. Chief Higgins took her away.

"I know it's Bruce, it just has to be. I just can't find the clue to snag him on," Pen said once they were gone.

"Often times there is none. Sometimes you just have to build as much of a case as you can and hope the jury can put it together enough to convict them. But let's not make any assumptions that Bruce is in fact the murderer. No use going down that road only to discover we've been going in the wrong direction the whole time. We follow the clues, Pen."

Penelope stood up straighter, her face brightening with a smile. "That's it! Oh, Richard, I could just kiss you!"

"What's it? Not that I'm objectionable to a kiss."

Penelope laughed, then rolled up on her toes to plant one right on his lips. She pulled away, grinning up at him like a fool. "I've been so focused on Bruce being the culprit, I was ignoring the clues that were right there leading directly to the real murderer: Morris Belmont!"

CHAPTER TWENTY-FIVE

Chief Higgins was rather preoccupied with Joan at the moment. Penelope didn't want to mention anything about Morris until she had confirmed the clues that led to him being the one who shot James.

"Care to tell me why it is I deserved that kiss? More importantly, how you figured out it was Morris who killed James?" Richard asked.

"Directions and locations. I mean, that's a small part of it, but just enough to make everything else work. Possibly. At the party, someone mentioned that they thought Morris was in Nantucket. I thought it was just the casual mistake of someone a little too ossified. His family has been in Newport for the last few weeks. What if he really was supposed to be in Nantucket? Perhaps he even told his family he would be, but came here instead."

"That seems a bit tenuous, but how does it connect to him committing murder?"

"I need to ask Savannah one quick question first just to confirm something," Pen said, taking Richard's hand and dragging him back outside where Savannah had now moved to the edge of the deck. Pen came to a stop, her brow wrinkled with worry about what Joan had said earlier, referencing *The Little Mermaid*. She hurried along even faster to the end of the deck.

"Savannah!" She slowly turned her head to look back at Penelope. "Are you alright? You aren't too upset about Finn and James are you?"

A mild smile came to her face as she pulled aside the wisps of blond hair the sea breeze flung in her face. "I know what you're thinking. No, I'm not that far gone, Penelope. I just...I needed time to myself, time to think about things."

Pen nodded. "As it turns out Joan was the one to steal my gun. She wanted to make Bruce look guilty. It wasn't the murder weapon after all."

"That makes sense. I thought it might be either her or Finn."

"Have you seen Bruce's collection of guns?"

"Everyone has. He loves showing them off."

"And where does he keep them?"

"In a locked cupboard in his room."

"Locked with a key? Not a combination lock?"

"Yes."

"So, easy enough to pick."

"I suppose," she said with a frown. "What does this have to do with James's murder? Do you have proof Bruce did it?"

"Actually, I think it might have been Morris."

Savannah looked understandably surprised. "Morris? Why would he kill James?"

"The night of Martha's murder, you were with James, correct?"

"Yes," she said.

THE GREAT GASTON MURDER

"And he was painting you that night? Out on the porch?"

"For most of the evening, yes, He finished it that night, thankfully. It was the last night of a decent moon before..." She trailed off without finishing.

"Right," Pen said, pausing before continuing. "So, just to confirm, that was the final night he painted you on the porch. Every other time you two met after that, you were up to other...endeavors?"

Savannah blushed slightly and pursed her lips. "What does this have to do with anything? Even if James had wanted to paint me after the night of Martha's murder, it was too cloudy. There was no moon, the light would have been off."

"So he painted you by moonlight?"

"For the most part, yes. We had a small candle as well. He always preferred painting me outside."

Pen felt her blood rush with fervor. "Just one more thing, Bruce mentioned some 'hullabaloo' taking place at the Belmont home, something Martha may have done. Do you know what that was?"

"As it turns out, their home was broken into. Considering everything I learned today, I can see how it may have been her, taking advantage of them being gone."

Pen exhaled with satisfaction. "Thank you for your help, Savannah. I think we may just be able to get him."

Pen grabbed Richard's hand and left an understandably confused Savannah staring after them as she rushed into the house and back out to his car.

"Okay, so like me you probably suspect Morris may have been the one to break into his family's home. I can't make the connection to him killing James," Richard said as he started the car.

"We need to go back to Sands Point and question the Belmonts. Don't worry, I'll explain along the way."

"At this point, I've learned to trust your hunches, Penelope. So what was it that first struck you?"

"It was Joan, actually. She used the word 'moony.' It made me think of something Morris had said earlier, describing James painting Savannah 'by the light of the silvery moon.'" Pen crooned the words to the song just as Morris had. "But it's been overcast ever since Martha's murder. In fact, I was worried it might rain the night of my party. If he had only arrived at Sands Point the morning after Martha was killed, as he claimed, how would he have known about James painting Savannah by moonlight, unless he'd seen it? We can check with Finn and Joan, but I'm certain her brother wouldn't have aired his family's dirty laundry by telling him, and Joan only likes revealing secrets if she can get a rise out of people. Morris wouldn't have cared about that. As for Bruce, he was perfectly clueless."

"But how does that lead to him murdering James?"

"Unfortunately, I think it was James himself who may have signed his own death warrant."

"How so?"

As they rounded the road to the other side of the bay Penelope told Richard everything that had been said when she and James had gone to visit the Carlton home.

"I swear you can narrate a scene as though I'm there," Richard said, shaking his head in wonder.

"For me, it *is* as though I'm there."

"Your talents are definitely a bonus in your newly chosen profession."

"And to think, I could have been a detective. Perhaps I should apply to the Women's Bureau. Do you think Isabella Goodwin would have me?"

Richard turned to face her in surprise.

"What? Do you think there isn't a modern woman in the city who doesn't know about New York's first female detective?" She asked with a laugh. "Going undercover as a maid to nab Eddie 'the Boob'? Twelve-year-old me was over the moon about it. I still remember that newspaper article I read, word-for-word."

"Well, you of all people could certainly finagle your way into the hideout for a gang the way she did. Your method always seems to follow the path of—"

"Meddling?" Pen teased.

"Indeed."

Richard turned onto the street where both the Belmonts and Carltons lived, both homes lining the water looking out at the bay across from Glen Cove. They stopped at the Carlton home first.

It was a bit of an obstacle getting past the butler this time. Even the reassurance that they didn't suspect Bruce of the crime didn't seem to work.

"Just tell him that if he doesn't talk to us right now to help us seal the case against someone else, we will be getting a warrant to search the entire home, which Mr. Carlton knows will do him no favors. In fact, we may uncover evidence that a prosecutor will be more than happy to use against him instead. One simple question is all we need to ask."

The butler closed the door in their faces, and Richard and Penelope waited to see if the reassurances and threats from Detective Prescott would work.

They were soon met by a very skeptical Bruce Carlton. "You said you had one question?"

"Has one of your guns been stolen, Mr. Carlton?"

A look of outrage came to Bruce's face. "I knew it!

You're trying to trap me again. If you think I'm going to fall for—"

"Oh for heaven's sake, we think Morris was the one to kill James," Penelope said, if only to shut him up and get him to cooperate.

"*Morris?*"

"Yes, but we need to confirm that your gun was stolen before we approach him."

He kept his mouth shut, staring at them with naked contempt.

"We can always get a warrant to confirm that it's missing," Richard said. "We won't be so willing to investigate our suspicions that it leads to someone else if you make us work that hard."

"I..." Bruce looked so conflicted, Pen almost felt sorry for him. Almost. He knew he was damned either way, so he, surprisingly, chose the correct path. He sagged before answering. "Yes, it was."

"That's why you thought Finn had also killed James?" Penelope asked.

"Yes, I thought surely it must have been him. But you think it was Morris?"

"When did you first notice the gun missing?"

"Not until we got back this morning."

"And the last time you saw it?"

"Yesterday morning."

"And I assume Morris has been in your house between then and now."

Bruce nodded, a bewildered look on his face, as though he was still trying to understand it all.

"Just to confirm, I assume you keep your guns loaded?" Richard asked.

THE GREAT GASTON MURDER

Bruce tilted his chin up defiantly. "There's no law against that."

"No, there isn't," Richard said with a sigh.

"The day James and I came to visit you, you said you had seen Morris drive in that morning?" Penelope asked.

"Yes—well, no. I saw him that morning. I didn't necessarily *see* him drive in per se. Finn and I were on the water, set to sail out that morning and saw him through the windows of his home. We got his attention and had him join us on the water. I couldn't tell you exactly when he came back to Sands Point."

"One final thing, you said there was some hullabaloo with his parents? Something Martha had done?"

"Yes, their home was broken into. It had to be her, no?"

"And when did Morris tell you about this break-in?" Pen asked rather than answering him.

"Yesterday."

"So he didn't tell you anything about a break-in before then, even though he'd been here at least two days before that?" Surely it would have been something interesting worth mentioning to a friend right away.

"No, he didn't!" Bruce said, finally catching on. "So do you think that Morris was the one to—?"

"Thank you for answering our questions, Mr. Carlton," Richard said, tipping his hat and turning to leave. Penelope followed him back toward the car.

"Hey, wait a second! So you think it was Morris who killed James? Answer me!"

Richard and Pen ignored his pleas, instead entering the car. They drove further down the road to the Belmont residence. This one was more befitting the coastal aesthetic of Long Island, large and white, done in Colonial architecture.

After knocking on the Belmont's front door, it was eventually opened by yet another butler. By agreement, Penelope allowed Richard to do the talking, at least to get them past the threshold.

"I'm Detective Prescott with the police." He wisely didn't reference which department he was with. "I'm here to speak to the Belmonts about the break-in that occurred this week."

"The police have been here already."

"Yes, I'm just following up. We think it might be related to another crime. Are they home?"

"Yes, of course. Please come in," he said, leading them into the parlor. "I shall go and get them."

"Please make sure Morris Belmont comes as well."

"Yes, miss."

While they waited Penelope studied the decor. It was understated in a way that Old Money loved, but she had a trained eye that knew how much everything was worth. Paintings that were originals, not replicas. Furniture that was precious antiques, not modern. Quality fabrics and fixtures made of precious metals. A field day for a thief who knew what to look for.

And Morris Belmont certainly did.

"You're here about the break-in?" A man's voice said, capturing the attention of Richard and Penelope.

Pen turned to see Morris's father, Clarence Belmont, walk into the room. His gaze fell on her and a crease of confusion formed in his brow as a slight flicker of recognition touched his eyes. Morris followed him in, but the confusion in his eyes was laced with cautious assessment as they landed on both of them.

"Yes," Richard answered. "I understand the police have

been here already. We're just here to follow up on a related crime."

"What's she doing here?" Morris asked, jerking his chin at Penelope.

"Miss Banks may have information related to the crime as well. She's here as a courtesy," Richard said evenly.

"Yes, yes, let's get on with it then," Mr. Belmont said impatiently.

"Can you tell us what was stolen from your home?" Richard asked.

"Two paintings, a silverware set, and some jewelry my wife left here. You stated this was related to another crime? Is it Martha's murder?"

"No, not that. It seems one of your neighbors, Bruce Carlton had a gun stolen. Now, and this is where we need your help, we think it may have been used in another murder."

"Is it about that business with a murder that took place at a party? In fact, I recognize you now, Penelope Banks. It was *your* party!"

"Yes, it was," Pen confirmed.

"I should have known. I've done business with Reginald, who always seemed like a practical, upstanding man. It's no wonder he cut you off."

"Mr. Carlton is claiming that it was your son who stole the gun," Richard said curtly. He needn't have worried about Penelope's feelings. She was quite used to criticism from the bluenosed set, even before her father had cut her off financially and socially.

"He's claimed *what*?" Mr. Belmont roared. "That's preposterous!"

"Of course, we agree with you," Richard lied. "We think Mr. Carlton is covering for his own actions. But we need your son to confirm as much so we can make our case against him."

"Anything you need," Mr. Belmont said, not noticing how uncomfortable Morris suddenly looked.

"He claims he told your son about the missing weapon long before the party, but Morris was in Nantucket this week—I'm sorry, Newport. That's correct?" Richard asked.

"No, it was Nantucket," Mr. Belmont said before Morris could answer. "He left on Monday to stay with his aunt."

"Actually, father, I left early and came here Thursday morning. I was rather bored with Nantucket. Pen knows this," Morris said, giving her an icy look.

"We still need more proof that Bruce shot James. The motive was obviously jealousy as anyone who was at the party could see. But before that, what reason would he have had to even know James and Savannah were lovers? Why would he have preemptively brought the gun to my party if he didn't know about them beforehand?"

Morris coughed out a laugh. "Come on Pen, it must have been obvious even to you. The way they stared at each other that day you came by?"

"James was an attractive young man, and Savannah is just as attractive. That doesn't really prove anything."

"What about the painting? The one of Savannah right there in the room at the time. Bruce knew James had painted it."

"Did he? I've seen James's most recent work in his cottage, and it looks nothing like that one," Pen lied.

"Don't be deliberately dense, Pen. If you've seen his most recent work, then you'd know James had been painting Savannah this whole time. As often as Bruce uses that telescope of his, he had to notice them as well. Even Bruce isn't that dense."

"Notice James painting Savannah?"

"Yes!"

"How do you know he was painting her?"

"I saw them myself!"

"By the light of the silvery moon?" Pen said softly. "Except, James had finished the painting the night of Martha's murder, which also happened to be the last night there was a silvery moon out for him to paint by. Save for the night of my party, thank goodness. That night, the sky was filled with fireworks, which you knew about ahead of time, thanks to my visit. The perfect thing to mask a gunshot."

"I...wait just one—"

"Not another word, son," Mr. Belmont interrupted.

"Probably a wise decision," Richard said. "Fortunately, we already have your fingerprints handy. I'm sure they'll match at least a few on the cabinet where Bruce keeps his gun collection. I'm also certain that if we do enough detective work, we'll find out where your son has been fencing all the stolen goods he took from your home...when he arrived at Sands Point earlier this week. Bruce has confirmed he didn't actually *see* you drive in that morning, you were already here when he sailed past."

"Blasted!" Mr. Belmont couldn't help from exclaiming. He turned to his son with anger. "What the hell have you done?"

"It's surprising what one sees that others fail to notice," Penelope said, staring hard at Morris. He snapped his gaze from his father to her. "That's what James said to you that day we stopped by. It's what made you worried that perhaps he had seen you here long before you claimed to have come to Sands Point. You probably saw him and Savannah out on their porch, maybe through the telescope that you claim even your home has. The light of the moon was certainly bright enough. However, you couldn't have him telling anyone he'd seen you here. So you killed him. And why not? After all, both Finn and Bruce had better motives. You could even avail yourself of one of Bruce's guns that he liked to show off so much, expert thief that you are."

"That's enough, we're done talking," Mr. Belmont said. "I'd like you two to leave. If you want to speak with my son, it will have to be with an attorney. Unless you plan on arresting him?"

"I think we'll leave that to the Glen Cove Police Department," Richard said with a smile. "After all, the murder was in their jurisdiction."

Richard and Penelope left the two Belmont men to stew in the "hullaballoo" Morris had caused. It was enough for Pen to know that she had discovered who had killed James. However, she would put all her resources into making sure Morris didn't escape justice. She pondered everything that had happened the past several days as she joined Richard back in the car.

"I know what you're doing," Richard said before he drove off, Penelope sitting silently next to him

"What?"

"You're going back through that mind of yours, wondering if perhaps you did something that may have contributed to his murder. Wondering if you had done something differently, even if only slightly, would it have made a difference?" Richard reached out to take her hand. "Going down that road leads to nowhere. It won't bring him back or change what happened. Trust me, I know better than anyone."

Pen recalled the story Richard had told her about his childhood best friend and what had happened during the war, where he had perished in a plane crash.

"I'm just sad I only got a few days with James, not even knowing that he was related to me."

"So, focus on those few days. Then, move on with your life. There's a lot of it still left to live, Pen."

She smiled softly and nodded. With one last searching look, Richard did the same, then drove them back to Glen Cove.

"Richard," Penelope said after several minutes. "Promise me that if we end up together—get married I mean, not that I'm thinking that far ahead—I know we both have troubled pasts when it comes to engagements, so I don't want to make you think—"

"I know what you mean," Richard said, staring ahead with a smile.

"Right," Pen said with a small laugh. "Just...promise me we'll do it for the right reasons. That you won't settle because you've found someone you're just fond of or feel safe with. I don't want you to see me as nothing more than an acceptable match or someone you respect but don't really..."

"Penelope," he said before she could finish. He pulled over to the side of the road and left the car idling and turned to face her. "That very first day I laid eyes on you, you... fascinated me more than any woman I'd ever met. Mostly it was the way you looked back at me, as though I was just as fascinating." His right jaw, the side with the scar inadvertently twitched. "Then I waited, waited for your expression to change, for it to sour into what the world usually greets me with: pity, disgust, curiosity. But it didn't. If anything you seemed nothing less than irate with me," he said with a smile.

"You have Agnes to thank for that. That and my misunderstanding as to your true purpose for being there. I simply thought you were an incompetent detective."

Richard laughed, then took her hand in his. "It's a testament to how good a detective *you* are; the truth above all else. And here's my truth, Penelope...dear. You still fascinate me. I suspect you always will. I'm never simply comfortable with you, and that's a good thing. I know that if I hitch my horse to your wagon, it will never be a smooth ride, and frankly, I don't think that's what either of us is looking for. But know this, whatever fire I have, and yes, *Penelope dear*, there certainly is a fire, I'll let you know well ahead of time if I ever feel it starting to fade." He studied her for a moment, an enigmatic smile on his lips. "Somehow I don't see that happening."

Throughout his entire heartfelt speech, Penelope felt her own heart quickening until it was likely to burst. Rather than any words, which would never do such a grand gesture any justice, she fell into him, pressing her lips against his. Oh yes, there was fire, intense, passionate, burning fire, and Richard met hers with the same heated ardor. When they finally pulled away, it hadn't faded.

Richard took a long breath, then spoke again. "That said, there are also all the boring and mundane things that make a relationship last, respect, fondness—

"Blather, blather, blather," Pen said, falling back into her seat with a smile and rolling her eyes.

"There's also frustration, exasperation, incredulity, pure madness..."

Penelope laughed and slapped him lightly on the arm. "As though you don't bring out the same in me." She tilted her head and smiled. "But yes, I respect you and I am quite fond of you too, Detective Prescott. Though, I'm too much of a proper lady to mention the exact temperature of my fire."

He grinned and turned to get the car going again. "We both know you're anything but. Still, who says I have any interest in a proper lady?"

"Now you're beginning to sound like my father. Speaking of which, at some point, I suppose I'll have to *formally* introduce you, rather than have you flying in with me to interrupt his day during the course of a murder investigation. I'm sure you're both rather weary of that."

"And at some point, you'll have to meet my parents as well. They're away until the holidays—teaching."

"Oh, is your father a professor, then?" Pen asked.

Richard paused, staring thoughtfully ahead as he drove. "Something like that."

"You make it sound so ominous."

"My parents are...well, I suppose you'll just have to wait and see." Which sounded no less ominous.

EPILOGUE

The Glen Cove police had placed Morris Belmont under arrest for the murder of James Gaston. Two of the party attendees who had been near James confirmed that they'd seen Morris near him at the time of the murder. They'd done a search of the property, eventually dragging the lake in between the cottage and the main house. That's where they'd found the gun used to shoot him. Miraculously, they'd found a single print as well, the same that matched those on Bruce's gun cabinet. They had also found the stolen goods, not yet fenced, sitting in a warehouse in Manhattan.

The trial would be a ways away. However, Morris, who had apparently felt the allowance given to him by his parents wasn't enough to satisfy his needs and wants, had suddenly discovered what it was like to be left without even that much. His parents were refusing to pay his legal fees.

The police had finally cleared entry into James's cottage. Penelope was with Savannah entering it for the first time the night of the murder. Now, they both stood before his final work.

"Yes, I can see how he improved," Pen said in wonder as she studied the painting of Savannah.

There were traces of the work Pen had seen back in the Carltons' home, but the strokes here were bolder and more confident. Unlike Degas, James liked vibrant colors rather than pastels. Savannah once again stared at the artist from the canvas. On her left stood a single candle, the orange and yellow casting its glow on her. Behind her, high above was the silvery moon, casting a different kind of light on the scene. And further back, across the bay in the distance was the familiar green glow that came from a single window.

"It was to be a wedding present," Savannah said with an ironic smile as she stared at the painting. "Something for me to hold onto as the promise of what we had planned. Bruce would have never been the wiser."

"Well, it's still yours. I'm sure James would have wanted it that way," Penelope said.

Savannah shook her head and a sad look came to her face. "No, I couldn't bear looking at it without feeling resentment. I have the only painting of his that I want."

Pen knew exactly which one she was referring to. It was the one James had done of her in Paris—the happiest two weeks of his life.

Savannah took a deep breath and turned to Penelope. "James had a will. I know he left me all of his paintings. He wanted to make sure his grandfather never received anything from him, even after his death. I'm gifting you this painting, Penelope, if you'll have it. Maybe it will have better memories for you. I know James wanted to tell you who he was, but he wasn't sure how it would be received. Please don't hold that against him."

"Of course I don't." Pen turned to the painting. "I wish

he had told me though. I feel I only barely got to know him the few days he was here."

"I would love to tell you all about him, everything I know at any rate. I'll show you his letters from Paris, well, most of them. It's where he was happiest. He didn't like to talk too much about his time in the carnival, understandably."

"I'd like that, perhaps we can meet regularly, as friends," Pen said. Her eyes fell to Savannah's bare hand. "I noticed you no longer have Bruce's ring."

"There's no longer any reason to marry him. I don't care about the money, and now Finn won't be needing it. His debts will just have to go unpaid. Bruce isn't happy about it."

"I imagine so," Pen said, unable to hold back a smirk at Bruce experiencing his own failed engagement. At least Penelope had done the jilting, which was more than he could say for himself. "So, what are *your* plans?"

A bright smile came to Savannah's face. "Me? I'm going to art school, right here in New York. My family would have never allowed it, of course. What happened to James has made me realize how important it is to seize what you want while you can. I only wish we had both done that rather than hatch this silly plan of ours. Perhaps then James would still be here."

"Don't think that way," Pen quickly said, placing a reassuring hand on her arm. "I'm sure wherever James is, he would be happy knowing that he at least influenced you to live your life on your own terms, doing what makes you happy. That's what you need to take away from all of this. Don't let his murder consume your thoughts."

Savannah nodded silently, then turned to the painting.

"He had so much talent. It seems a waste for him to be gone so soon."

Penelope put her arm around Savannah. "Well, the nice thing about art is that it allows the artist to live on forever, even after they're gone. I'll happily take the painting, and give it a place of honor. I'll look at it and focus on the brief period I got to spend with the cousin I never knew, the happy memories."

They stared at the painting a moment longer, then Pen squeezed Savannah's shoulders. "Come, let's go inside. I'll make us some French 75s to drink in James's memory. I think he'd appreciate that."

Continue on For Your Free Book!

GET YOUR FREE BOOK!

Mischief at the Peacock Club

**A bold theft at the infamous Peacock Club.
Can Penelope solve it to save her own neck?**

1924 New York
Penelope "Pen" Banks has spent the past two years making ends meet by playing cards. It's another Saturday night at the Peacock Club, one of her favorite haunts, and she has

GET YOUR FREE BOOK!

her sights set on a big fish, who just happens to be the special guest of the infamous Jack Sweeney.

After inducing Rupert Cartland, into a game of cards, Pen thinks it just might be her lucky night. Unfortunately, before the night ends, Rupert has been robbed—his diamond cuff links, ruby pinky ring, gold watch, and wallet...all gone!

With the Peacock Club's reputation on the line, Mr. Sweeney, aided by the heavy hand of his chief underling Tommy Callahan, is holding everyone captive until the culprit is found.

For the promise of a nice payoff, not to mention escaping the club in one piece, Penelope Banks is willing to put her unique mind to work to find out just who stole the goods.

This is a prequel novella to the *Penelope Banks Murder Mysteries* series, taking place at the Peacock Club before Penelope Banks became a private investigator.

Access your book at the link below:
https://dl.bookfunnel.com/4sv9fir4h3

ALSO BY COLETTE CLARK

PENELOPE BANKS MURDER MYSTERIES

A Murder in Long Island

The Missing White Lady

Pearls, Poison & Park Avenue

Murder in the Gardens

A Murder in Washington Square

The Great Gaston Murder

A Murder After Death

A Murder on 34th Street

Spotting A Case of Murder

The Girls and the Golden Egg

Murder on the Atlantic

LISETTE DARLING GOLDEN AGE MYSTERIES

A Sparkling Case of Murder

A Murder on Sunset Boulevard

A Murder Without Motive

ABOUT THE AUTHOR

Colette Clark lives in New York and has always enjoyed learning more about the history of her amazing city. She decided to combine that curiosity and love of learning with her addiction to reading and watching mysteries. Her first series, **Penelope Banks Murder Mysteries** is the result of those passions. When she's not writing she can be found doing Sudoku puzzles, drawing, eating tacos, visiting museums dedicated to unusual/weird/wacky things, and, of course, reading mysteries by other great authors.

Join my Newsletter to receive news about New Releases and Sales!
https://dashboard.mailerlite.com/forms/148684/726783564877673718/share